THE UNFOR GETTABLES

GL TOMAS

Copyright © G.L. Tomas
Published by Rebellious Valkyrie Press

First paperback edition September 2016

Cover Design by Najla Qamber Designs
Copyediting by Little Pear Editing
Formatting Design by JT Formatting
Comic Design by Alice Bessoni
Illustration by Geneva Benton

Library of Congress Cataloguing-in-Publication Data is available

ISBN-13: 978-1-943773-13-8

To discover current and future publications by Rebellious Valkyrie Press, check out our official website (http://gltomas.net/)! If you want awesome book recommendations, or just want to talk books, join us on our review sites Twinja Book Reviews (http://twinjabookreviews.blogspot.com/) or Rebellious Cupid Book Reviews (http://rebelliouscupidbookreviews.blogspot.com/)!

To all the geeks, nerds, weirdos, and kids
(including adult-kids like us)
that broke the mold even when no one saw it.
Your magic is real.
Don't let anyone tell you otherwise.

1

ME ZANMI!

PAUL

Moose crossings, lobsters, and lighthouses. That was the most I had to look forward to in this new place I'd now regretfully call home. Thank goodness I had my own car. I would've died had I been crammed into a backseat of my parents' with both Micah *and* Kevin for eighteen hours straight.

Like most eight-years-olds, Kevin wasn't so bad when he had an iPhone to keep him busy. What was most distinct about him was how young he normalized his non-conformist demeanor. Kevin wasn't sure about anything, but he liked femininity just as much as he liked being a boy. He loved My Little Pony, painting his nails, and took pride in taking both the mother and father roles whenever he could convince our parents, Micah, or me to play house with him. I remember my parents having the talk with Kevin when he was six. They let him know it was ok to be who he wanted, even if that was someone different than who we'd been nurtured to know, but his answer from then until now never changed. *I like being a boy; I just like other things too.*

Micah, on the other hand, was only good in small doses. She thought she was so badass since she was starting sixth grade this year. I wouldn't call Micah a genius, but she reveled in the fact that she was ten times smarter than me at her age. *Heck, in life in general.* But everything about her was just an attempt to outdo me. I shaved the sides of my hair; guess what she does? I take up dance and drawing, she just has to one-up me by nearly getting skipped up a grade, so everything I did looked small in comparison.

Needless to say, I was glad I rode with Kevin. He slept half the ride until our first pit stop, ensuring he wouldn't provoke my short temper. My parents preferred Micah ride with them. "She's not our favorite. She's just the most useful," My dad might say.

Being the oldest always had its challenges. My siblings were young enough to make new beginnings and adaptable enough to not miss as much about our old home like I would. I'd spent my whole life in Chicago. All seventeen years of it. When I packed, there were constant reminders of what I was leaving behind in the only home I'd ever known. My friends, my dance group, my world; all to move here.

To Portland, Maine.

A place in the middle of nowhere.

Maine was what I'd heard described as the whitest state in the country, and seeing it now, I could totally see why. I mean, they actually have signs...*for moose crossings*. Not exactly something I'd make up. My mom wouldn't stand out around here; she was blonde and averaged height. She looked like anyone just passing by. But Dad, Micah, Kevin, and I...well, we didn't look white.

Thinking back, where I'd grown up, I never thought about race too much. I'd had a diverse pool of friends, and no one personally ever made me feel out of place. I was lucky I guess, but even with the most genuine intentions, I was faced with a question like *"What are you mixed with?"* from someone you'd just met that day in your quest to score a "Welcome to New Hampshire" magnet made me again miss the melting pot I was leaving back in Illinois. I'll probably never get used to that. The same way I'll never get used to blueberries. Oh...I just might use that as a new swear word.

A light tap flicked on the outside my room door. It was open, so mom walked right in. "It's almost six o'clock Paul," she reminded me. I didn't forget, but we'd just unloaded everything from the move, which took hours, by the way. "I'll be right there," I said, stretching to my new bedroom door.

The living room didn't have the luxury of being precisely arranged the way my perfectionist mother would deem as a balanced living space, but it already smelled strongly of rosemary incense, my dad's favorite because it reminded him of Italian food. I stood in front of the statue of Buddha and prompted to bow three times. The pitter patter of feet and Micah's laughter echoed in the room as Kevin darted past me, but not after Micah bumped into me.

I ripped around, pointing at the demons. "Dad, seriously. Get them. *Geez!*" I rolled my eyes and had to start all over again. A crackled *blueberries* left my throat as I lowered my head to the ground as my first act of puja.

Dad managed to wrangle up the devils as my mom sat next to me and took one of my hands. She closed her eyes. "Observe your breath first then start with the Three Refuges," she said, breaking contact.

"How come Paul always gets to do the Three Refuges?" my brat of a sister Micah asked. Dad gestured for Kevin to sit across on the opposite side of mom as Micah crossed her arms over her chest. "You get to do the offering Micah; Paul's better at the chants. Behave."

I stuck my tongue out at Micah. *Brat.*

It was the second day of summer and already my mom had found a way to remind me why I'd rather be at school instead of home all day.

"Felicia Bijou Abelard, I did not raise you to be this lazy," she said in a heavy Haitian accent at the opening to my bedroom door. "When I ask you to do something, it is not optional. Me zanmi!" she exasperated, referring to the mountain high pile of laundry I should've done hours ago.

"Maaaaa, relax. I'll do it right now. It's summertime, you know; I'm in bum mode." I passed her on my way out my room. She patted my hair as she occasionally did when she was seconds away from making a comment about it.

"And when are you going to fix your hair, eh?" I rolled my eyes.

"Never, ma, Never," I mumbled. Because to her "fix" meant straighten, and I liked my hair in the big, puffy awesomeness that it was. It'd only been two years since my big chop, and I'd already reached bra strap length. I most certainly did *not* miss lye relaxers and hours of precious time wasted with a flat iron.

She followed me to the basement to make sure I didn't throw any colors in with the white stuff. My mom was wearing pink shirts for a week the last time I did laundry, and since then, she always made me put the clothes in one by one. *Talk about annoying.*

"Ma, can I have a few dollars to go to the tag sale the Richardsons are having?" I didn't know what it was between me and tag sales, but I'd always managed to score the coolest stuff.

Last year, I'd found the perfect green trench coat to complete my genderbent rendition of Sazh Katzroy from Final Fantasy 12 to wear to PortConMaine, and just a month ago, I'd walked away with the complete, original game Valkyrie profile for PS1, mint, for ten bucks. Ten bucks! On eBay, that game sold for no less than one hundred.

"You buy all this stuff you don't need. What happened to all the money that Tante gave you for your birthday?"

See, what my mom failed to understand is that my birthday was ten and a half months ago. I didn't know a person alive that can hold onto a hundred bucks for an entire year when you had a penchant for all things Avatar. That glider replica I bought depleted nearly half the funds, and a girl had to have her luxuries. I wasn't anywhere close to completing my Korra costume for next year and was pretty sure I wouldn't have enough saved to go into Boston to get my hair braided. That dream, as of yet, would have to be put on hold.

My mom must have gotten bored watching me put the clothes in the washer; she was already on her way up the stairs. I threw the last cup of detergent we had in the load and turned the dial to start it up. In four quick steps, I'd caught up to her, ready to be the fly by her ear until she forked up the dough.

"Ugh, Felicia. Pran sa'a!" she said as she handed me a crisp twenty-dollar bill from her purse. "Now go. Shoo!"

I yelled a quick "Thanks, ma", making my way to the garage to get my bike. Normally, I'd use my two feet. Where we lived in Portland was made for walking, but I had to hurry before all the good stuff was gone. That and there was no way I was missing that Teen Wolf marathon at noon. Oh summer, how I love thee!

2

HiTBOY/SLASHGiRL

FELiCiA

I dismounted my bike, a little bummed that there were already six other people fishing through all my future treasures. The Richardsons had a gigantic lawn and from first glance, I counted eleven odd some tables of potentially useless junk. A lot of the traffic scoped out the tables topped with china and silverware, but I had my eyes set on what most people didn't want.

I made my way to one of the vacant tables decked with shoes, hats, and seasonal things like heavy coats and even a pair of gloves. One of the jackets was pretty nice, but it was the end of June, so the last thing on my mind was keeping warm. *On to the next one.*

I passed a few spectators bearing waves and good mornings to familiar faces. There was a table filled with some kitchen appliances that looked almost brand new. My guess was these people never cooked because even the newest pot and pan set at my house looked used to death. Had to give it to my folks. For people who both worked full time, how they found the energy to cook every night was beyond me.

Unless I was washing dishes, everything I did in the kitchen was nothing short of a catastrophe. I definitely did *not* inherit my parents' skills in the culinary arts. I didn't know what I'd do without them when I was away at college. *Probably starve. Yea, that's right, I'd probably starve.* I wonder if they were selling any cookbooks?

"What do you think? Think green's my color?" the boy standing next to me asked, holding up a green Boy Scout textile badge to his face as he smiled. I'd never seen him before, which was odd because around here everybody knew everybody. His hair was shaved on the sides with the only length being on top and slicked back. The side of his neck that was visible to me was home to a small tattoo that looked like written words in Sanskrit, and his style was super trendy in an urban-meets-hipster kind of way.

Because Portland was such a lily-white town, it wasn't hard to forget the few people of color when I saw them. He didn't look fully East Asian, but I'd say he was at least part something. It didn't matter. All I knew is that he was the cutest boy I'd ever seen in person and not just Portland-cute but big city boy-cute. Chances were, he wasn't from around here, and I'd never ever see him again. *Bummer.*

I walked over to another table and almost didn't notice that he followed me until our hands touched while reaching for the same pile of comics, and not just any comics, but a stack of the rarest, most underrated comic book series ever to hit the market: HitBoy and Slash/Girl. It was the first comic I'd ever read where the superheroes were more like a tag team rather than a hero and sidekick. I know, totally rare for boy/girl pairings. There was only a 2,500 print run, and while I'd read all ten copies online, it didn't replace having the real-life, actual masterpiece in your hand. This was about to get ugly. *Fast.*

"I take it you're a fan?" he asked through a clenched-teeth smile, never lifting his hand from mine. He had beautiful hands. Long, pale fingers with well-trimmed nails.

"Fan? Try HitBoy and Slash/Girl devotee. The term fan is beneath me." Sure, he was cute and everything, but there was no way I was leaving this table without these comics in hand. This was war.

"Who did Slash/Girl consult when she lost her superpowers to the solar eclipse?" he asked without taking a breath. Boys were always accusing you of being a fake fan of anything they held dear. To be a fangirl in this day and age, you had to get used to all the condescending comments, all the insults and the million and one questions guys asked to prove how knowledgeable you were about particular fandoms. I hardly bought into it, but if there was one fandom I was highly versed in, it was the Amazing Adventures of HitBoy and Slash/Girl.

"Ha!" I shot back. "SlashGirl sought advice from her mentor 'The Sonic Wave'. *Duh!*" I said triumphantly. "Where did HitBoy go after he passed the seventeen trials of Mythogon? Since you're *such* a fan."

"Okay...umm, that didn't happen," he stated. "You're just throwing things in there to trip me up...but it's cool. It's obvious you'd appreciate them more than I would." He lifted his hand off mine and suddenly, my bare hand felt lonely.

"They're yours." His eyes were a warm shade of brown with hints of amber that would make anyone stare too long just to appreciate how pretty they were up close. Note to self: break eye contact.

"You like comics?" he asked, snapping me out of my zone. It wasn't that I was the biggest fan of comics, but what I liked, I liked. He nodded in understanding.

"Yea, I wouldn't say I'm the biggest comic book fan either, but I'm drawn to the simple storytelling. It's amazing how some stories can be told in just images with minimal words. Plus, I like to draw, so I don't know, they're just awesome to look at."

I didn't want the conversation to end, but I had to find one of the Richardsons so I could complete my transaction before he changed his mind and wanted to King Solomon me for this rare find. My total came to nine dollars. It meant I'd totally have enough for a mid-afternoon ice cream binge. *Sweet.*

When I turned around, mystery boy was gone and possibly forever out my life. Maybe I dreamed him up. I wouldn't put it past me. It was almost eighty degrees outside and the humidity was murder. I really needed that ice cream. It was a good thing I didn't walk. Maybe a guy like him was too good to be true; otherwise, what would he be doing talking to me? Yeah, for sure a dream. *Oh well.*

I waved goodbye to all the new people who showed up as I moseyed on over to my bike. Next stop, the supermarket.

A horn beeped at me the second I hit the third corner. A blue Prius pulled up to the sidewalk and as the window rolled down, and I'd abandoned my initial thought because it became perfectly clear. It was him! The guy from the tag sale. I didn't make him up.

"See you around Slash/Girl," he said with a smile before pulling off into the road. He *was* real. "See you around Hit-Boy." The Illinois license plates made me weigh the chances as very slim, but it brought a smile to my face, thinking of the possibility.

3

DINNER DATE

PAUL

"**K**nock, knock."

I don't know why my parents ever knocked. It was more a formality than anything because they always walked in anyway. Taking a few days to finally settle in, I'd made it my mission to stay attached to my bed the rest of the day.

"What's up, Dad?"

"Don't make plans. We're eating over a neighbor's house," he rushed before I objected.

"Since when?"

"Since like, forty-five minutes ago. Figured you'd be happy not to eat leftovers."

I rolled over on my bed, dangling my feet to the floor. "Do we all have to go? Why can't you and Mom just go?"

"Paul, I can guarantee that without a doubt, that whatever you're doing right now is not *that* important. Come on, this'll be a good time to get to know our neighbors. You never know, we might need them one day."

I couldn't possibly think of any ways complete strangers could come in handy for the future. "Like what?" I asked with a tone of sarcasm.

Dad shrugged. "*What*? Do you want me to come up with something on the spot?" A long drag of silence fell between us. Dad knocked his knuckles on the wall before walking out and leaving with, "Just be ready at seven. Thank you!"

He could've at least entertained his argument with "they have a bomb shelter" or something. I liked meeting new people, but neighbors were a different case altogether. *Please don't let them turn out to be weird.*

It was just a few feet away, but the walk to the front door felt like a mile. From the outside, our neighbors lived in a really nice house. There was a stone pathway leading into the backyard with a large collection of plants and flowers growing up from the soil that bordered the house.

"Ugh, Dad. Why do you have us dressed up like dweebs just to eat dinner?"

Dad was holding mom's vegan pound cake, trying his hardest to tear the bratty siblings apart from their back and forth bickering.

"Paul, they seemed like classy people. I didn't want to make a lousy impression. Besides, all you did was put on a bowtie. I hardly think that qualifies as 'dressing up.'"

Maybe I was just looking for something to complain about. But I kept my mouth shut when Mom knocked on the door. When I didn't notice any movement in the house, I peeked inside the living room window. Squinting between the blinds, Mom rung me at the collar, smacking me on the back of the head.

"You don't just look inside people's houses, Paul. What is wrong with you?"

I rubbed my head to soothe the pressure. "Ouch. I was just seeing if anyone was home. Are they Haitian or something; there's a Haitian flag in the hallway."

Dad shrugged and spoke through gritted teeth, "I don't know. It's not like I asked. That's rude."

"How is that rude? People ask us that all the time!"

Dad's eyes darted to Mom. He always looked to Mom when we were inadvertently talking about something either one of them found awkward or impolite to bring up.

"I'm going to let you handle this one," was one of his go-to lines for it. Mom patted down Kevin's cowlick, shooing Dad away like she always did. They mumbled back and forth about pointing fingers, and my dad's famous *"He gets it from you"*, was an argument Mom could almost never win. The name on the mailbox read "The Abelards". In a sea of awkwardness, the door finally opened.

A dark-skinned black man in a button-up, tie, and slacks stood at the door. He had a gentle smile and kind eyes and honestly looked like he'd just gotten off of work or something. That or maybe he was just fancy. My dad was in his sweats the moment his briefcase hit the driveway.

"Claude, so nice to see you again!" Dad chimed, forcing a smile, as *Claude* held out his hand to shake.

"I see you got your whole gang here with you," Claude said.

"Yeah…well, I couldn't just leave them while I stuffed my stomach. Claude, this is my wife Robin." Mom extended her hand and gave a light greeting before Dad moved on. "

These are my kiddos Micah, the good kid. Kevin…the questionable one, and Paul, the teenager." As Claude reached out to shake my hand, his grip was light, like he wasn't used to shaking hands.

"Oh, we have one of those too," he joked. "Paul is it? How old are you, Paul?"

I shrugged. "Seventeen."

"I have a daughter about that age. But she's a little anti-social. She's in her 'I'm too cool for school' stage. She only comes out when there's food to be eaten or gifts to be given. Maybe you'll meet her, though. If she isn't being grouchy." She sounded cool already.

Dad intercepted before I could say anything stupid. "I'm sure she's lovely. If she attends Deering, I'm sure they'll cross paths a lot."

"Why don't you all come in and make yourselves comfortable? My wife had to pick up something from the store, but we spent a bit of time preparing vegetarian options for you guys."

Mom and Dad took turns explaining our dietary restrictions. "Sorry to be so picky, it's just…we're Buddhists, and we prefer not to eat meat. We hate that you went out of your way to accommodate us." my Mom said.

Dad laughed. "You really picked the short end of the stick when we invite you guys over for dinner; I'll tell you that!"

Mr. Abelard and my Dad shared a laugh at his corny attempt at humor. I thought my Dad told the worst jokes, but people always laughed at them, so all it did was convince him that he was actually funny.

As we walked to the living room, through the hallway, and finally to the kitchen, the fragrant smell of spices became hard to ignore.

My parents' cooking never smelled so alive! Mom was a total health freak, so we didn't eat anything containing gluten, limited amounts of sugar, and a whole lot of other things if she could help it. Dad? Let's just say when he cooked, he wasn't best at sharing it with the rest of us.

"Do you have any other kids?" Mom asked as she pulled out a chair at the table for Micah and Kevin.

"One in college, but he's doing some traveling over the summer. So you may not get a chance to meet him until the holidays. Paul's just a year younger. Maybe the two of you would get along?"

I faked a smile. I'm sure Mr. Abelard meant well, but I wasn't looking to be someone's play date. I'd make friends in my own time, even if it meant waiting until school started.

There was a table set up, and I counted eight chairs, so I was curious as to who else was joining us other than Mrs. Abelard.

"Dinner'll start the minute my wife gets home, but in the meantime, I'll go get my daughter." He wasted no time yelling her name out loud.

"Felicia! Would you come on down; dinner is about to start."

I sat between Mom and an empty chair, while Dad sat next to Mom and closer to the kids.

"Okay, just give me a second. I was trying to get to a save point on my game. I'll be like five minutes." They went back in forth in a language I couldn't begin to understand, but I'm guessing it was Kreyol because that's what most Haitians spoke. *I think.*

The rush of footsteps resonated as someone descended from the second floor, and when the girl walked in, my mouth dropped. *No way.*

"Slash/Girl?"

"HitBoy?"

Dad looked between the two of us, gesturing over his chair. "Well, at least you guys know each other!"

"**W**ell, I wouldn't say any of us would qualify to be poster children for animal rights. We just don't believe an animal's sole purpose was to be on a person's plate. But that's my personal opinion. I can't speak for everyone; I can only speak for me," Mr. Hiroshima finished calmly.

When Mom got home, dinner started right away. Dinner took a lot longer than usual, but I hadn't known why until now. Mom was so used to frying everything in pork fat, including

Diri Ak Pwa—a rice and beans staple in Haitian cooking, that Dad argued it wasn't really vegetarian. As a last minute option, Dad prepared his house famous Legume. I loved meat, but between the sweet chunks of chayote and slices of plantain in a rich tomato-based stew, my mouth watered at the way the carrots, beans, and cabbage soaked up all the flavor. You couldn't even tell you were eating something that didn't have a mother.

Since fate has a funny way of keeping you on your A-game, it turns out HitBoy was part of the family who moved in after our past neighbors, the O'Connors, put their beautiful house up for sale a few months into the school year. Okay, so his name wasn't *really* HitBoy; it was actually Paul.

We hadn't talked that long at the tag sale, but here he was, sitting right across from me at my dinner table. It was getting hard to breathe. He was more than just cute; he was charming. And now I had to live with the fact that he lived right next door.

Stuffing my face seemed like the easiest thing right now. I didn't want to give away that I liked looking at him; otherwise, my parents would never let me go near him. They were strict enough as it was, but as far as they knew, the only boys I had crushes on were in comics, graphic novels, in books, or on cartoons. I was fifteen, but they treated me like a kid.

"So, what would make you become a Buddhist?" Mom bluntly asked, directed at Paul's mom, Mrs. Hiroshima.

"I'm afraid I don't know what you mean," Mrs. Hiroshima laughed. Mom's aggressive hand gestures, something she often used for yelling or speaking in Kreyol, suggested she was trying to ask something bluntly but didn't wanted to offend.

"Well, you know? *This*!" Mom pointing at his mom, making her even more confused than before.

I decided to rescue the conversation and get to what she was *trying* to ask. "I think she wants to know because you're White." My mom was a cross of well-mannered but direct at the same time. It wasn't really rude to point out obvious things where she was from, so often, I was afraid that sometimes she came off as a little offensive. I was always saving her from making it worse, but despite it feeding her curiosity, she really meant no real harm by her inquisitions.

"*Felicia*!" Dad grunted.

"What? I bet she wouldn't be asking if she wasn't." Paul held his hand to his mouth, shaking his head. He was bad at holding his laughter as he leaned in to say something to his father. "Dad, they're so hilarious."

I hoped the curve of my mouth didn't look like a smile. No one ever thought I was funny before.

"Well, I can certainly assure you that I didn't become a Buddhist because Mike is. We honestly met at a Buddhist retreat in college. Mike was non-practicing, and I was born Episcopalian, but as I explored other spiritual paths, Mahayana just seemed like a bit of a calling for me. It's worked well for me so far," she ended with a chuckle.

Daddy had this look on his face like he wanted to do damage control, but he, too, was so interested in our neighbors' differences, it was all they could talk about.

"We sincerely apologize if we're making you feel uncomfortable. We don't know anyone who's Buddhist and never have. It just brings up interesting conversations, that's all."

Paul finally stopped laughing and looked over at me. Suddenly, my plate became the most interesting object in the room.

"Well, we hope you don't form your opinion on Buddhism as a whole, just by meeting us. There are several different branches, just like any religion, and if I'm being honest, we're fairly liberal with faith," Mike said, as he finished his plate.

Dinner was almost done, and like an annoying boss, Mom whipped her hands toward me to fetch all the dirty plates off the table.

"Oh, I'll help you," Paul said as he stood and took plates on his side of the table. I decided to take my time so I wouldn't bump into him and make a fool out of myself.

Mom and Dad were still busy probing Paul's parents with questions like they'd never met people who weren't Haitian or Christian before. I think they were curious because they were Christian, and it didn't make sense to them not to be Christian. They were pretty tolerant, so the questions were just to make sense of everything.

"Oh, you know how it goes," Paul's dad interjected in the background, "we try not to make too many worldly attachments to things, but I keep saying *tell that to my mortgage!*"

Paul and I were inches away from the kitchen sink when he hunched over laughing. In a low voice, he whispered, "That's like the twelfth time he's told that joke. He pulls it out his pocket whenever he thinks the conversation calls for it. He thinks it's so funny."

I fought hard not to smile, but it wasn't easy. I didn't have any girlfriends; hell, I didn't have *any* friends. Sometimes, it was just nice to laugh with someone who didn't know a lot about me and could judge me based off what they knew and not what they'd heard. Maybe the moment wouldn't last, but for now, I think I liked the idea of Paul being my next door neighbor.

Mom and Dad served the pound cake that they brought over in the living room after dinner. I wondered what made it *vegan* since meat wasn't actually in cake, to begin with. I would've been locked in my room, praying our other neighbors would've gone home by now, but being this close to Paul, I didn't want him or his family to go.

He sat next to me on the loveseat, far enough to where I wasn't freaking out, but close enough that I noticed all the tattoos on his wrists, neck, and the space under his ear. He wasn't your typical seventeen-year-old guy; he was actually cool. He must've been lucky. Counting up all his tattoos made me resentful that I wasn't even allowed to wear makeup yet.

"Hey Ma, maybe I should become a Buddhist. I'd be able to get tattoos and piercings in more than one place." Paul's parents laughed as my fossil Mom rolled her eyes and Daddy shook his head.

"Here we go again," he muttered under his breath.

"Felicia, take in mind, we don't just let Paul *do* what he wants just because we're of a different faith. We have rules just like any house does. Since he follows most of them, *notice how I emphasize most,*" Mike stopped to gesture to my parents, "we just give him certain freedoms to express himself the way he feels comfortable."

Dad chugged a sip of his Ji Papaya, a delicious fruit smoothie made with evaporated milk, before going on about how much I disappoint him as a daughter.

"Well at least if you went that route, you'd believe in something. This one over here is an atheist." My dad pointed towards me.

Paul's parents' faces said it all like they were going to have an interesting conversation about this when they got home.

"Well…that's definitely an interesting conversation starter. And I'm assuming by your candidness, that you two are not," his father asked.

"Eh! Sa'a fou. She is just confused," Ma said, throwing her hands up in the air. Paul turned around, pressing his back against the couch, literally an inch away from my face.

"Is it more that you don't believe in organized religion or that you don't believe in God?" he asked, his warm brown eyes, sparkling with flecks of amber.

"I don't know. It's kind of a little bit of both, I guess. It's a longer conversation than just taking the easy route out and throwing me under the bus like I'm the Antichrist."

"Well, I don't know about you, but I'm a bit exhausted talking about religion all night. It was nice to have an intelligent dialogue about it, but can we talk about something else? Maybe more interesting, like Edwidge. You mentioned being from Haiti, right?" Mrs. Hiroshima spoke, resting her hands in her lap.

Ma smiled, beaming with pride. If anything could put her in a friendlier mood after discussing my religious choices, talking about her first love, Haiti, was one of them.

"Yes, I am originally from Port-au-Prince, but I've been living here over thirty years. "

Mrs. Hiroshima and my mom found common ground once they brought up traveling, since she mentioned visiting several Caribbean countries, but never being lucky enough to visit Haiti. Paul tapped me on the shoulder, but my attention was already on him, even if he'd only just noticed.

"You've got to let me borrow those comics sometime."

"Well, you already know where I live. I'm sure we can take turns hoarding them, you know since you did kind of let me have them. As long you, ya know? You go through the proper protocol and stuff." And then he giggled. *At something I said.*

"You're really funny, Felicia. Dinner definitely wasn't a drag because of you guys. You probably won't like the food as much when you come over our house, but maybe we can hang out sometimes, just in general. I doubt you'd be into the stuff I'm into—"

"I don't know. I might surprise you," I said, a light smile forming. He smiled back.

"Maybe you will."

It was the longest, yet most entertaining dinner we'd ever been invited to. And now that I knew Felicia lived next door, I'd be swimming in those HitBoy+Slash/Girl pages in no time.

The Abelards were actually pretty nice. Mr. Abelard reminded me of my dad, but ya know, actually funny. And Mrs. Abelard? Well, the thing most distinct about her was that she was so unbelievably tall. She towered over my 5'9" frame with heels, and did I mention how insanely beautiful she was.

She sort of looked like she could have been a model back when she was young, but assuming she was around my mom's age, she was still ten times more glamorous and put together than my mom or any of my friends' mothers back home. Plus, she was generous with all the plates she allowed us to go home with. My mom rarely let us go back for seconds, but in our defense, my folks cooking was never good enough to go back for additional servings.

And then there was Felicia.

Even when I'd approached her earlier at that tag sale, I kept thinking that there was no way my first real drive around Portland would result in me meeting someone that awesome. Even from far away, she was really, *really* cute. She had perfect skin, smooth and dark brown, free of the scars and blemishes that had plagued my arms and legs from injuries and roughhousing over the years. Her eyebrows were thick and so perfectly arched that it added a mystery to her nearly black eyes. And her hair was a hypnotic mass of curls and kinks that made me want to take out my sketch book right then and there.

From underneath my mattress, I pulled out my sketchbook, flipping through dozens of portraits until I reached an empty page. Working out my proportions, with soft lines, I traced Felicia's face shape in my head. Oval-shaped faces were always a little challenging for me, which is why I usually started with a 2B pencil. The lines were light to start, and I could always go a little darker with harder strokes.

For me, it was hard to resist drawing a new face. She was pretty, and not just attractive, but symmetrical. I found it difficult to draw someone accurately the less physical imperfections they had. I loved finding reasons to replicate kinky hair. Tighter curls were interesting to draw. I had fun mapping out the layers and textures it took to really make it pop off the page.

Mom and Micah both had uneven cheekbones, while Kevin had a gap between his teeth and a scar on his lower lip from playing around too much. Dad had a wider nose bridge, a nostril smaller than the other, and don't ask me why but had a slight crease in his left eyelid, whereas the other one didn't. Even I had different facial bone structure and what I considered a blended eye shape since I inherited two different phenotypes from being both Japanese and Welsh.

Flipping through the pages, I saw sketches of my parents, my siblings, even a few great grandparents whom I'd never met but immortalized in pictures.

People's wrinkles, crow's feet, crooked teeth, their imperfections...They were all traits you could bring attention to what would make an imperfect sketch, perfect.

"Oh, you got my crow's feet," Mom would say. "I look super fat in that," Dad might joke. But Felicia? My portrait of her might never really look like her. Her face was too perfect. I could draw her a thousand times before I got half her face right.

But it was cool to have someone new to draw. Really cool.

4

THE UNFORGETTABLES

FELICIA

Okay, so watching the boy next door flipping around shirtless in his backyard isn't creepy at all, right? Maybe if I'd spent the *entire* half hour watching him in his cocksure, yet entertaining, grandstand play of gymnastics, it would've been. But no, I've taken snack breaks, the lamb out of the freezer just like Ma asked me to, and my hair from last night's twists. *I mean, it's not like I've been watching him the whole time…*

Who am I kidding? I've left my post for a total of two and a half minutes, and it wasn't like I needed to look away from the window to separate my curls. I was becoming that neighbor: the kind you regretted introducing yourself to because you were never prepared to deal with their antics. Tia and Tamera had Roger. The Winslows had Urkel, and The Wilsons had Dennis the Menace. I wonder what my nickname would be?

Why did the people moving in next door have to have a teenage son? And why did he have to be cute? If he was going to Deering in the fall, there's no doubt he'd be popular, which meant any chances of us being friends beyond the summer were next to none. High school was just an insignificant stain in my so-called life. I couldn't wait to graduate. That's when the fun started. Or at least that's what I've been promised.

For now, I'd decided that spending my afternoons spying on the neighbors' seventeen-year-old son was time well spent. And just when I thought this summer would be eventful like the last two.

"Felicia! Why are you just sitting around in the house all day doing nothing?" Mom screamed. I jumped up so high that if it hadn't been for my hair, I probably would've hit the ceiling. She laid three bags of groceries on the counter, yelling at me in Kreyol (where everything always sounded more serious and urgent) to get the rest of the bags from the car outside. So much for snooping on the boy next door.

I stepped outside only to be assaulted by the summer's thick, muggy air with no means of escape. Just the walk to the car was like walking across the Sahara with no sight of people or water for miles. I would definitely be staying inside for the day.

"Hey." Paul crept up behind me, looking super cute in his board shorts and loose-fitting tank.

"Hey," I answered back. I was terrible at saying the right things. It was best to keep it simple.

"Need any help?" he asked with a smile. It took a lot of effort not to snort or choke. "I mean if you're going to offer..."

He took half the bags from my hand, and together, we made our way into the kitchen.

"Hi, Mrs. Abelard," Paul declared with a smile.

My mom returned the gesture, looking as though she hadn't been yelling at me just moments before. Ma rarely smiled with genuine interest, but my guess was that she really liked Paul. The only other times I saw my mom smile was when she bragged to my aunts in Connecticut about how smart I was. My mom loved to have the leg up when chatting with her sisters how successful their kids would be. Despite my brother Jonasen being away for college, so far, I was in the lead.

"Et comment ca-va?" Ma asked.

"She means, how are you?" I said with a roll of my eyes. My mom was always finding excuses to be someone's foreign language teacher, and while I was grateful for being conversed in more than just English, it was annoying always having to translate when people had no idea what she was saying.

He laughed.

"I'm fine. Just might spend the afternoon finding some place to eat around here. I'm starving." Before I could object or put my two cents in, Ma offered my assistance, and if I knew my mom well, she wouldn't tolerate a "no" when she so politely promised someone something.

"Why don't you let Felicia show you around. I'm sure she knows more places than we do; she's always walking around. Let her show you."

Paul turned in my direction with an anxious look on his face like he felt my discomfort.

"You don't mind?" Just like Ma to mess up my plans in attempts to keep all the air- conditioned goodness to herself.

"Sure, C'mon. I already know a spot I know you'd like."

I don't know how I let Felicia talk me into what would have been a ten-minute drive, into sightseeing all around Portland on our bikes. I didn't even own a bike; I had to borrow one of her older brother's bikes that wasn't very comfortable, but in her defense, it'd been a long time since I'd ridden a bike, so it could have been all me. Her argument was that there were places she wanted to show me I'd never appreciate in the driver's seat of a car. I begged to differ. The entire drive here, I did nothing but look around in wonder.

Nowhere in Chicago we ever lived was this green, this peaceful, or this clean. I didn't need a bike tour around Maine to see that.

Felicia turned back to let me know we were close to the restaurant. After this long ride, I had plans to order the whole menu.

It was a hole-in-the-wall spot with yellow brick walls and tables so close to each other that just an inch to the left, the table next to us could have basically been part of our party. I chose one of the lone tables by the wall, so at least it'd be just the two of us. I had my eyes set on the Peanut Curry while Felicia ordered the Thai Ginger Noodles. At least that was quick.

"So ummm...weird question. Have you ever eaten meat?"

I shook my head. Being a vegan wasn't hard at home. My entire family didn't eat meat, so there was no adjusting anyone's diet.

Now, my friends, they were harder to be around when we got hungry. My friend Beto's family was from Puerto Rico, so to him, being vegan meant that meat was just served on the side, and my other friend Kenneth was Filipino. Even some of the soups his folks made had meat in them. It was nice to meet someone who went out of their way to find a place that we could both enjoy.

"I mean, it's hard to miss something you've never had." She nodded in argument. Her phone rang, and she answered it, yapping off in the same language I didn't quite understand. Made me envious that I didn't speak another language.

"Sorry," she said after she hung up, "just my mom reminding me not to stay out too late. *Parents*," she added before sticking out her tongue. There was something sort of whimsical about Felicia, and I liked that.

Most of the girls back home were afraid to be themselves around guys, as if they needed to be perfect all the time. Felicia seemed different. Like being someone other than herself wasn't an option. Being pretty was nice (*And she was definitely that*), but being yourself was just about the coolest thing a girl could be. That, and her hair was awesome.

"So tell me; what's Deering like? Starting school as a senior, not exactly on my list of ideal situations." She rolled her eyes and faked a smile. "Deering's great...if you're a pod person."

"C'mon. It can't be that bad."

"Oh, but it is. Aside from people being fake and phony, Deering High students have unknowingly discovered ways to silently torture me. I mean, if there was a contest for how many times a person could hear 'whatever' or 'dude' or 'oh my god' at the start and end of every sentence, Deering High students would definitely take that one home."

The waitress returned and laid down two moderately-sized plates of some of the most amazing food I've ever sunken my teeth into. This would, for sure, turn into one of our go-to spots.

"At my old school, it was super lit. I mean, if you like arts and that sort of thing. I met most of the guys I used to dance with there, and I swear the dancers...we *so* owned that school. It sucks starting all over."

A small pit of sadness formed in my stomach. Chicago was the only place I ever knew as home, and now it was obvious that I wouldn't be graduating with my friends. She smiled wide across from me, instantly brightening up my mood. She had the whitest, most perfectly- aligned teeth and a pretty smile that made me think of what more I could say to keep that curve on her mouth from fading. Was I getting too ahead of myself? After all, we only met a few days ago. But already, I knew that her friendship was something I wanted…

"What kind of dance do you do?" she asked as she took a sip from her Thai iced tea. Anytime someone asked me that question, it was like I'd lost all control over my limbs.

It started at my fingers. They operated in a geometrical way that moved in sync with the music playing in the background as my arms formed isolations that no doubt told a story. I was into most styles, but tutting, a hip-hop skill set with close ties to popping, was my absolute favorite. My folks had put me into extreme martial arts to be more social and make more friends, but once I started dancing, I'd found something I loved more than tricking. Like drawing, dancing was my life.

"Okay, so you just became ten times cooler. I can barely manage a milly rock. You'll totally stand out at Deering. Everyone there is probably just as pathetic and rhythm-less as me," Felicia said. I laughed.

"You're not exactly selling it," I said, taking a hefty bite of curry-infused tofu. "I guess the bright side is I'll know you," I flirted. She cringed.

"Yea, fair warning. That might not be a good thing."

Before I could ask her to elaborate, the waitress approached us with an army of refills and a series of small talk that forced us to switch the momentum of where our conversation was headed.

"Hurry up and eat already. There's this place I want to show you before it gets dark."

With that, I stuffed my face with whatever was left on my plate and even skipped dessert. Felicia offered to go half on the bill, but I refused. I didn't want to come off as cheap, and I was glad she'd taken the time to get me out the house all day. Although seeing as how I only had a couple hundred saved up, I would need to look for a job soon. For now, I just wanted to enjoy the time I'd have with a new friend.

"C'mon, Felicia. Let's see this place already," Paul said as he led me by the hand impatiently to my planned destination. We'd left our bikes a few miles back and walked the rest of the way to my special spot. A place I'd never taken anyone to.

The land belonged to an elderly couple, The Phillips, a family that my father used to housesit for. I'm pretty sure my dad used to work with Mrs. Phillips or something, but they had an amazing, cozy cabin that they let us vacation in during the summer. My parents weren't ones to vacation in a place that only took twenty minutes to drive to, but I liked spending time here. It was so serene and peaceful.

"Wow, this is so cool." He followed me inside, eyes wide with excitement at the glossy cabin-grade walls. "And the door was just open?" he asked. I shrugged.

"No one really locks their doors around here. That, of course, isn't an invitation to start turning door knobs or anything. Just felt like I should mention that."

"This place is so sick!" he said as he made his way to the glass sliding doors that looked out to their private lake. "Is it okay if I get a closer look?" he asked with pleading eyes. He looked like a cute little puppy scratching on the front door, waiting for someone to walk him. How could I say no?

We rushed outside and he surprised me when he took his shirt and shoes off. Totally not looking. Okay, so it was hard not to look, but I promise I didn't stare.

Paul's body was lean, not overly muscular for his height or build, but typical for your average seventeen-year-old boy. There were some cuts here and there, two tattoos between his ribs and back that weren't visible to me from my peeping tom session back home. Being this close to a shirtless boy who wasn't a family member was tying knots in my stomach. He gave me this mischievous look before grabbing my hand, pulling me closer to the water. "We have to go in."

I anchored my feet to the ground, but it was no use; he was so much stronger than he looked.

"Wait, Paul, wait. I don't want to get my hair wet." He suppressed a few laughs before finally attempting to be serious.

"Understandable, but c'mon; it's like ninety degrees outside. Your hair will dry in no time."

Easy for him to say, with his straight, predictable hair. If I got mine wet, there was no telling what it'd look like an hour from now with no access to coconut oil and my detangling comb. Nope. I stood firm in my decision.

"It's okay, Paul. Swim your heart out. Don't let me stop you from having fun." He nodded and for a second, I was impressed with how well I'd handled my answer. That is, until he picked me up and hoisted me over his shoulder, taking off running toward the water.

"Nice try. But you're not gonna just sit there while I have all the fun. My motto is, seek forgiveness, not permission."

I was submerged in a pit of water as Paul lost his grip on me as I sank deeper into the waves. For once, I didn't regret my mom pushing me on those swimming lessons a few years back. I swam to the surface and was met by a laughing Paul.

"You should have seen your face." I, for one, was not amused. I spit out water my mouth, collected from the plunge, into his face. He continued to laugh until finally, I joined him. How could I stay mad at someone who could take pleasure in laughing at themselves? Still, he was going to pay for getting my hair wet.

"You're going down for this, you know that right?" I said, splashing water his way. His face flinched when the droplets entered his gold-flecked, amber-brown eyes.

"Felicia, this lake is awesome. Did you really only bring me here for us to just look at it?" Hearing it out loud only confirmed that that's exactly what I'd done.

"So, I was thinking we should name this place. You know how in HitBoy and Slash/Girl they have the Lair of Secrets? This could be ours." While the thought sounded promising, I was at a loss for what names sounded cool for our new potential summer hideout, silently freaking out that he included me in his future plans for this place.

Technically, it wasn't a secret, but as far as I was concerned, it was the perfect place to chill without my folks breathing down my back. Plus, the Phillips loved me. They were always excited to see me utilizing the place whenever they paid a surprise visit to their third home.

"So, I already have a name: The Unforgettable Spot."

"Wow, how original," I said coarsely.

"The twist being, the location of the lair always changes, making it super hard to infiltrate our secret hideout. We'll be like Hitboy and Slash/Girl. A duo." Can't deny he had an imagination. I hated to admit he'd had my attention.

"So, I've spent a whopping three minutes coming up with an alias sick enough to fully encompass everything that is amazingly me, so from here on out, I will be known as The 8th Wonder," he said in a dramatic voice-over kind of way. I was laughing so hard, I wanted to cry.

"So what are your powers?" I continued the façade. It was actually sort of fun.

"That's easy. I was born superhuman, so speed, strength, and agility. That's nothing to me. Opponents tire themselves battling me because I forgot to mention that I also have the power of duplication. Why do you think they call me The 8th Wonder?"

I knew where this was going, but I asked why, just to hear him say it.

"Because I can split and be in eight different places at once. Oh, that, and I can fly. Okay, you're up. I need a partner in crime; think fast. What's your secret identity?"

I was no good at thinking on the spot. With the pressure on, I blurted out the first thing to come to my mind, "Sidekick Supreme." He frowned before splashing water in my direction. Hair will be dry in no time, my butt. "Oh, c'mon. Sidekick Supreme? We're supposed to be a team, remember?"

I laughed, knowing that my decision needed some sort of explanation.

"You're obviously not seeing the bigger picture. As Sidekick Supreme, I am the queen of all sidekicks. Imagine every ability you've ever seen a sidekick have. Well, I have them all—superhuman intelligence, flight, wit, stamina… Not to mention, I can create force fields. I'm basically a superhero in waiting."

He looked slightly impressed with the breakdown of my awesomeness, and now we just needed a team name, one that signified when we were both present on the scene. Something that unified us, like the Justice League or X-Men.

"I got it. Together, we can be known as The Unforgettables." When I thought about how quiet my summers had been before Paul's family moved in next door, I'd come to the decision that in the two times I'd encountered him before today, I'd replay them over and over in my head so that I wouldn't forget them. The only word fitting for this summer so far was 'unforgettable.' His eyes watched me, considering.

"The Unforgettables? Definitely has a ring to it. I'm already seeing what this could be in my head." He smiled.

I had no clue what he'd meant by it, and unfortunately, I was too afraid to ask but, it was settled. From here on in, we were The Unforgettables.

5

VILLAINS LIVE AMONGST US

PAUL

A random call changed my life today. Or at the very least, my money situation. As soon as we'd moved to Maine, it was no secret that I'd been on the hunt for a part-time job. There wasn't a grocery store, pharmacy, restaurant, or shelter I hadn't applied to. In fact, I was even open to babysitting at this point because I couldn't function without my own money.

Mom wanted me to work for *everything* I did, which was fine. But allowance wasn't anywhere near the funds having a job would get my hands on. The only problem was *getting* a job. I had job experience, so that wasn't the issue. I don't even think it was getting the interview. Filling out job applications was the worst part.

Online applications were easier because I could take my time and could rely on a keyboard. Some of the places around Back Cove were old school, so they required paper applications. It wasn't so bad if I had a few to practice on, but I was often too embarrassed to ask for three.

Today, it didn't matter anyway. After a bust from some Italian restaurant, who wouldn't hire me because I wasn't eighteen a month ago, I'd finally gotten a call back from Shaw's up the street, and they wanted to know if I could come in tomorrow. I was too desperate to say no. Especially since I knew if I could get the interview, I could get the job.

But there were a few underlying issues.

Problem One: No gas

Granted, it was right up the street. When I mean up the street, more like a mile away, onto a main road. But should I *not* get the job, I'd look job-ready enough to apply at other places, which would waste more time without my wheels. But then there was another issue.

Problem Two: No money

Which was my fault. Since I'd had a job back home, I never had to ask my parents for money. Since I never had to ask, I got to spend what I earned on what I wanted. Nothing ever drained my bank account more than clothes. My mom usually sneered at that, in that passive-aggressive way she's used to. *"Paul, only you could spend a yuppie's budget and still look like a hipster."*

Which wasn't far from the truth. A slick combination of sporty, street, and edge didn't always come cheap. I did like deals, but it wasn't uncommon for me to spend two hundred and fifty bucks on a jacket either. Now, I had to order my clothes online since none of the malls around here suited my taste.

But having a strong sense of style didn't help me. I spent the summer running through the three hundred bucks my grandpa gave me as a going away present, so I was broke. I needed this job. I wanted to be able to put gas in my own car, but without a job, it left me with my last issue.

Problem Three: Asking my parents for the money

There was no way I was asking Mom. But Dad? Maybe. But it was best to consider him at the last possible minute. If I gave him too much time, he'd just suggest I figure out another way or ask Mom. It was best to ask when vulnerable.

I knew Dad had a weakness for Gelato Fiasco, which was great for him because we now resided in the very state it was created. When you bought it from a grocery store, you were limited to the freezer pints they sold. But my Dad almost lost his marbles when he took Micah, Kevin, and me to an official Gelato Fiasco store. With a vault of fifteen hundred flavors, I thought Dad was going to need medical attention and require being carried out on a stretcher.

After a little trial and error, he'd narrowed his favorites down to an avocado-orange (which tastes just like it sounds) and a sriracha-peanut combination (which for what's in it, is surprisingly tasty). To beat the heat, he never let the freezer be without one, and he'd have a serving of it every night. Of course, if he bought it for himself, it was meant for his mouth only. Which was why, after dinner, I'd help myself to a few scoops.

All I'd have to do is know how to play it, and five bucks could be mine. I'd even pay him back with my first paycheck.

My interview wasn't until two, and it was just my luck that Dad took a half day for a doctor's appointment. I showered, got dressed, and did everything I had to do before approaching Dad in the kitchen. He was playing a whack crossword puzzle, but Dad liked that kind of thing, so I felt bad for calling it whack.

"Hey, Dad? Think I could borrow five bucks for gas until a week or two from now?"

Dad took a sip from his Bard coffee cup. He vowed never to touch Starbucks again after having their brew. "What do you need five bucks for? Didn't your grandfather give you three hundred bucks before we left?" Of course *he* wouldn't forget.

I rubbed the back of my neck nervously, hoping to look more pathetic so he'd give in. "It's been like two months. I wouldn't ask if I didn't need it."

"Well what do you need it for?"

"I have a job interview in like an hour, and I just realized I don't have gas in my car."

Dad went to the usual, *What would it look like if I gave you money every time you asked? Do you think money grows on trees? Maybe if you didn't spend so much on clothes...* Basically all Mom's influence.

"I could walk there, but I was kind of hoping if I didn't get it, I could job hunt while I still felt like it."

Dad just shook his head. "Look, I'd just give you the money, but you know how your mother gets. You'll appreciate your car a lot more if you have to earn your own money to use it. Maybe this can be a learning experience," Dad said, assuming he'd just given the most profound advice. I knew when to quit when I was ahead, but I figured if I only had one option in my disposal, it was best to use it now.

I hugged around the corner and pretended to come back. "Hey Dad, I think I might have eaten some of your gelato last night. It was like, two a.m. and I was tired, but in major need of a sugar rush. I thought it was the sorbetto. My bad." I quickly turned the corner and hightailed out of the house when I heard the freezer door open.

Since coming into my powers and assuming the alter ego The 8th Wonder, it was amazing how painfully unaware I was that villains lived among us. My Dad? I'd had the honor of seeing how his decisions often only benefitted me when they, too, benefitted him.

His alter ego: The Opportunist.

I wasn't even down to the sidewalk before Dad raced out the door, keys in hand for his car. "I'll drive you. Just be ready by the time I get back." He wasn't stupid. Dad might've been suspicious of my timing, but even he couldn't resist his only vice. It wasn't five bucks but at least I had a ride.

I felt as confident as I could be during my interview that it hadn't surprised me they'd hired me on the spot. Starting to-day, I officially had a job. By next week, I'd finally have the cash I so desperately needed. I already owed my dad a carton of ice cream, excuse me, *gelato*, and that didn't even count the twenty I owed my little sister the last time I took the rascals out to eat at some place I knew was way out of my price range. My sister was a vault when it came to saving money; I was even considering opening up a private account at the United Bank of Micah. Man, this job came right in the nick of time.

There was a stack of paintings I started but put on hold because the fact was, I didn't have the supplies to finish them. Starting ten projects at once also contributed to this; either way, art supplies never lasted too long in my possession.

My phone rang in my pocket, and I was psyched to learn it was one of my friends back home initiating our third video call since moving here.

"Hey Dad, can I turn the music down?" I asked, already in the midst of doing so. As the call connected, a smile lit up my face to see that it wasn't just one of them. Both of my best buds, Beto and Kenneth, joined in on the call. They were literally the Larry and Curly to my Moe.

"Hey guys, what's up?" From the looks of the goings-on in the background, they were somewhere around the old studio that we all danced at. If I wasn't at school or work, my folks could almost guarantee I was at the dance studio. I pretty much lived in that place. I prayed there was a place like it in Portland.

"Everybody keeps asking what it's like in Maine," Beto said on the other side of the screen. All our other chats were always about old times, current twitter beefs, and how these two knuckleheads were holding up without me. It was the first chance I had a chance to tell them about my new home.

"I don't know; it's okay I guess. Quiet. That sort of thing." Kenneth pulled out his cell phone and focused on the screen with narrowed eyes as he scratched his cheek. I knew that look all too well.

"Yeah, so I Googled that place, and it said something about Maine producing ninety percent of the country's toothpick supply. I'm never gonna look at toothpicks the same again." No matter how far away my friends were from me, they always had the ability to bring up the stupidest stuff to make me laugh. Man, I missed these guys.

"So, you know what I'mma ask now, right?" Beto asked next. If I knew Beto well enough, the question was going to be about girls. Every August since we were thirteen, his parents sent him to Loiza, the place in Puerto Rico where they were from to tighten up his broken Spanish, but somehow by the grace of some higher power, he'd always claimed to have hooked up with the hottest girl on the island by the month's end. Kenneth and I both knew he was the world's biggest embellisher, but we never called him on it because the lies were always entertaining.

"How are the girls?" See what I mean? Like clockwork.

"You do realize my dad is sitting right next to me." I directed my phone's camera to my driving father, who at the red light thought it was a great idea to replace a "hi" with a poor excuse for the cabbage patch (who even does that anymore). And if that wasn't bad enough, threw in a series of equally embarrassing pops and locks. If I hadn't grown up with these guys, I would have been publicly humiliated.

"So, what d'you guys think? This old man got enough swag yet to try out for your dance crew?" On the other side of the screen, Beto fell to the floor laughing while Kenneth slapped his knees, gasping for air. After a moment of realizing how amazingly corny my dad was, I joined in soon afterward. Times like this made me forget I was so far away from home.

"Dad, please," I started as I pinched my nose and caught my breath. "Never repeat the words *swag* ever again. I'm begging you."

But I knew it was too much to ask. He'd only find other ways to force me to discover if divorcing a parent was possible.

"Besides, it's taken me weeks to find a job. That's all I've been focused on since the moment I got here. No chicas."

It wasn't a lie; I wasn't out here looking for girls. Not far anyways. There weren't "girls", just *a* girl. And we were just friends, nothing they'd be interested in hearing or making an announcement over.

"Ahh, while you were in your interview, son, your mom called me to tell you the neighbors invited us for a night on the town, so we're going to need you to babysit."

The burden of being the firstborn meant that it didn't matter how much I pleaded or how far in advance I planned, when Mom and Dad needed me to play responsible older brother, I had no choice.

"Aww, c'mon Dad. I made plans. Me and Felicia were going to go see that new Underworld movie. I've been telling you for days." Although thinking about it, I felt really bad since Felicia had offered to pay since she knew about my lack of cash. I'd only realized my confessional mistake when it was too late. I hit the end call button on my cell phone screen to shield myself from the onset of questions my friends would most likely ask me after my Dad and I settled this. I did tell them there were no girls after all.

"Paul, you have the whole rest of the month to see a movie. We parents, you see, we have these things called responsibilities that from time to time we want to get away from. You look forward to the entire summer; that's a whole two-and-a-half months you get to power down, but *we,*" he said pointing to his chest, "*WE* look forward to just a few hours out. Only *we* have to go to work the next morning. Let us have these few hours, son. Let us have this few hours."

He pulled into our driveway, looking confident that no matter what tricks I had up my sleeve, tonight was not happening. Or at least for me and Felicia, it wasn't.

"Here's an idea. Why don't you just see if Felicia wants to come over here. That way you can have an extra hand at handling the rugrats—I mean, your brother and sister."

His eyebrows rose to the middle of his forehead with a questioning gaze.

"Plus, it's free son. You can't beat free." Dad did have a point. With funds running as low as they were, it didn't hurt to have a movie night inside instead. I just hoped during my parent's absence, Micah and Kevin wouldn't give me too much trouble. *Yeah, right.*

"**He**y Mom, good news; I got a job today," I said entering the kitchen, ready to butter her up with the favor I'd planned to ask. Dad had already said no to my plea for five bucks, and I knew I'd have to present a reasonable proposal to my mom if I was to ask for even more than that. Mom wasn't moved by compliments, but I did get her attention every now and then when I took an interest in the reading materials she made me go over for the summer. Always a teacher first.

"I was looking at some of the exercises you left on my bed. Some are better than others, but I'm sure I could make use of them all." She took a break from her oven cleaning to look over at me to smile. Now that she was in a good mood, here was my chance.

"So, Mom, you think I could borrow like thirty bucks until I get paid. There's this place I wanted to order food from tonight, but they only take cash."

The Stone Glare. This woman had a list of fatal abilities, but her deadliest and overall most powerful was one I'd deemed "The Stone Glare". With just a look, she could turn anyone into a statue, not to mention the countless list of paralyzing powers she had at her disposal. When words left her mouth, they were not to be argued, and it was evident that she was the ring leader of all things oppressive.

Her evil secret identity: The Dictator.

"What's wrong with what we have in the house? I just went shopping, Paul. What did I tell you three about being so wasteful? There's plenty to eat in this kitchen," she said as she blew her short, blonde bangs out of her eyes.

While there was no way to deny my mom made a generous trip to the grocery store, I feared that everything we had to eat in this house would be too much of an adjustment for Felicia since we didn't eat any meat or dairy products. The Abelards had done an excellent job at catering to our needs; I just wanted to show her the same courtesy.

"But what if she doesn't want to eat any of this stuff?" I picked up a bag of Raw Kale chips and stuffed a handful or two in my mouth. These were actually pretty good.

"Honey, I know it can be hard to make friends when there are slight differences in the way you do things, but anyone who doesn't like you the way you are may not have any real interest in being your friend."

With her ring and middle finger, she pressed into my forehead and pushed me away. I suppose I should add superhuman strength to that list of abilities.

"Felicia's a sweet girl. Seems very open-minded. Better get cooking," she said, wagging her eyebrows. I hated when she did that.

Since Mom and Dad left, these two have been nothing but a pain-in-the-butt. Between Micah spilling an entire pantry's worth of cake batter mix on the kitchen floor and Kevin deciding that now was the time he wanted to give his old sled a test drive down the staircase, landing square into Dad's one-of-a-kind ceramic Pac-Man lamp, it felt like a scene in The Hunger Games. I was ready to kill these two. That lamp was older than I was, and I knew I'd see my last day if I didn't find a way to glue this thing back together.

"You guys better not think about trying to cook something without coming to get me. If you're really that hungry, just eat some of the casserole Dad made from two nights ago. Open anything else, and I'm calling Mom." Kevin looked to my sister for a list of instructions but when was offered only a nod, he retreated to the basement until there was further damage needed to be done. Sometimes he was on my side, others, he went with the best deal. For that, he couldn't be distinguished as a friend or foe.

His sobriquet: The Shapeshifter

Micah showed no fear at the sound of my threats to call Mom. It was an unsaid fact, but Micah was the favorite.

"By the way, I'm having a friend over. She just texted me a few minutes ago. She's a few blocks away," Micah said like it was no big deal.

"Mom didn't say it was okay to have friends over, Micah. As soon as your so-called friend gets here, I'm driving her home."

We stood face-to-face in a one-on-one staredown. She smiled from the corner of her mouth in a way that reminded me of the reason I hated being the oldest. Even if the wrecking crew I'd known as Kevin and Micah burned this whole house down with next to no signs of my contribution, I'd still get blamed for it.

My sister knew this and took full advantage of it. With heightened intelligence and the power to manipulate minds on her side, there was only one name fitting for this one.

Her moniker: The Prodigy.

She formed her hands into a steeple, and for a second, I thought the next words that would leave her mouth would be "Excellent" a la Mr. Burns, but no; what she said next was far worse.

"You won't be doing anything, or else Mom'll find out about that post office box they don't know about. Where you get *all* your college applications sent to. Word to the wise, you might not want to keep those out in the open. I just saw them on your bed when I was looking for some mousse. Kind of defeats the purpose of having one if people know about it," Micah said.

With what dignity I had left from her destroying me with that last comment, I stormed off to my room, the door slamming behind me. I fell back on my bed, crushing two large manila envelopes in the fold of my back.

"Stupid sister always going through my stuff," I mumbled. I had to find a place to hide this stuff, or my mom would go ballistic that so far, the only colleges I was interested in applying to were art schools. In the midst of deciding that under my mattress would serve as the best place, my door swung open behind me, unleashing a need to staple one of these kids to the wall.

"What did I tell you about just coming in my…" I started. Felicia stood at the opening of the door, her arms pinned to the back of her.

"I'm sorry. Micah said I could just come in. I'll just go out to the living room," she said as she lowered her chin to her chest and walked out into the hallway. *Nice going, Paul.*

"Wait," I said, trailing after her. "I thought you were my sister. I didn't mean to yell at you. C'mon."

She followed me back to my room, and I shut the door behind me.

"Sorry, it's just been a crazy night. They always drive me nuts when my folks go out, which I should be thanking you for. Thanks for not having better control over my parents, "I joked. "Parents going out on a weekday is unacceptable. I expected better from you, Sidekick Supreme. Tsk ,tsk, tsk." I crossed my arms over my chest, shaking my head slowly from side to side.

"Leaving me for dead is not what I call teamwork." A smile lit up her face that provoked a smile from me for putting it there. Felicia had the prettiest lips I'd ever seen and the pinnacle of smiles.

"Oh, don't be a sidekick, 8th Wonder," she carried on the act. "Must I be there every time to save your hide? There are hopeless citizens in dire need of rescuing. When I was in line for choosing useful powers, to avoid coming off as a copycat, I overlooked the ability to be in more than one place at a time; didn't think I'd ever need it."

One of the things I liked about Felicia was she wasn't afraid to be silly. A little geekery never hurt anyone. Especially coming from an insanely pretty girl like Felicia.

"Guess what I have..." She brought her hands from her back with all ten issues of HitBoy and Slash/Girl lingering in her grasp. I thought she'd been teasing me when she said she'd let me borrow them. Good to know she followed through on her promises.

"Is it okay if I hold onto them for a little while?" I liked to take my time since I wasn't a fast reader. "I'll give them back when I don't need them anymore. I promise." Satisfied with my answer, she nodded. I lifted up the corner of my mattress to place the issues underneath.

"Umm, is there a reason you're putting them underneath there?" I shrugged.

"I guess keep anything I don't want anyone finding here. It's cool, this is like the only place no one ever looks, and by no one, I mean the two brats in the living room." She strolled across my room, settling on one corner that gave home to rack full of trophies I'd earned back in my EMA days.

It'd been years since I'd entered a tricking competition. Once I'd discovered dance, martial arts had taken a backseat. But you never really forgot how to "trick" when you've been doing it at long as I have. It was definitely still a part of me.

"It's so cool you have so many trophies. I always wanted to get into cool stuff like that, but of course, my parents wouldn't let me. Thought I'd get hurt or whatever," she said with a roll of her eyes. "I'd probably be like, Ultra Sidekick Supreme by now if my parents didn't suck so hard."

She picked up a few rough sketches I'd laid out on my work desk, and I silently cringed since they weren't that good. In spite of that, I never threw anything away just in case I went back to it and made something interesting out of a mistake. It didn't happen often but still, it happened.

"Did you draw all these?" I nodded. "You don't under-stand how amazing these all are." As she shifted through my work in progresses, I was grateful that my portrait sketchbook was nowhere in sight. I'd started a handful of pages of her face alone. If I were her, I probably would have thought it was creepy to find portraits of myself drawn by someone I didn't know well, but in my defense, I drew almost everyone I met if I could remember what they looked like to me.

"Your room is exactly how I envisioned it." She looked around in wonder. Other than my artwork and a few trophies, there wasn't much to my room. Its layout was pretty simple. But my closet, that is where things got complicated. I wasn't raised to form attachments to things, but clothes were another way I expressed myself. My style was a little bit of Chicago, a little bit street, but definitely all me.

"Oh, I like this symbol. I'm so jealous I can't draw." She held the sketch up to her chest and I smiled. They were some 8th Wonder concepts, and I knew it was really cheesy, but I was really into this secret identity thing. My friends and I all had dance nicknames, but being an "Unforgettable" had pushed me into mapping out my own wannabe comic strip with my sobriquet, The 8th Wonder, as the title character.

But of course, procrastination and writer's block were my two best friends, so the symbol I drew was as far as I got with it. A loud crash followed by the cries of my hyper brother traveled to my bedroom, and all I could find the energy to do was sigh.

"Mind if I go check on them? They're probably just hungry or something." I snapped my fingers when I remembered why Felicia dropped by.

"Oh, look through some of the streaming services we have. My Dad pretty much has all of them, so there has be something comparable to what we were going to see. If not, we can just rent something."

Another thud sent me running into the hallway, hoping I could salvage what was left of this house after my brother and sister got done with it. If there was anything left.

Obviously, I hadn't known Paul long, but from what I gathered in the weeks of meeting him were that his skills as a babysitter were in definite need of a makeover. While I had no younger siblings of my own, getting kids to listen to me was kind of my specialty. After witnessing what seemed like the most painful ten minutes of my life, I silently excused myself to a trip to my house's garage.

The hoard of lawn chairs we had made it difficult to see the items I was in direct search of. I squeezed past a corner of boxes stacked to the ceiling and pushed past the lawnmower until a box labeled "Fanal" finally came into view. I hoisted it up with all my strength as I carried it back to the Hiroshimas.

I slipped my shoes off at the welcome mat, kicking the door shut with my foot and followed the sound of the trio's back and forth squabbles.

At the time of our family's first dinner together, I couldn't help but think the three of them looked like an edgy co-ed version of the AJR, with nearly identical hair styles. My mom had a huge debate about me going natural, but she would've never let me shave the sides of my head. The three of them were lucky to have parents that let them experiment with style.

In the corner by the counter, there was a girl Micah's age with short blonde hair, eyes glued to the floor. I could have sworn she wasn't there a minute ago, but maybe I hadn't noticed her since the three of them argued in the kitchen as if at war for the last Tickle Me Elmo doll come Christmastime. All eyes were on me when I set the box, I carried in my arms, down on the kitchen table.

Kevin, who was a foot shorter than me, jumped up and down in an attempt to see the box's contents, but it was Paul who stuck his hands in first. He pulled out an assortment of heavy duty brown paper bags, some soup cans, and a tube of acrylic paints, a grimace adding to his confusion.

"What is all this stuff?" I winked, but it was more of a cheesy wink. Comical, even.

"Stick around and you might get to see."

Ma had taught me so many cool things to pass the time on a rainy day. Guaranteed to grab any suspecting child's attention. Now, I most certainly had theirs'. Helping myself to a pot from a lower cupboard, I brought a few cups of water to boil as I mixed a cup of flour in a separate bowl of water. Once it was mixed to my preference, I poured it in the pot of boiling water, letting that, too, come to a boil before removing it from the front burner to then add a generous amount of sugar.

"Don't tell me you're baking," Paul teased. I stuck out my tongue.

"No, it's what I need to make the newspaper stick to the cans. It's like papier-mâché paste but a lot cleaner." The artist in him nodded, which made me wonder if he'd ever gotten messy with projects that required more than a pencil and sketchbook.

While the mixture cooled off, I invited the other girl to sit at the table with Paul's siblings, and although she was a bit quiet than anyone I was used to, I did hear a few please and thank-you's as I showed her my mom's weaving technique on how to make a braided bracelet out of yarn. She was better at it than the other two were. They kept growing impatient, tangling up the yarn and having to start all over again, trying to get the hang of the intricate lacing it required.

I looked up from my own masterpiece to find Paul gesturing for me to meet him in the hallway. Kevin and Micah stayed, too immersed in their crafting to pay me any mind.

"You, Felicia," he began, pausing dramatically in between, "really are hella-supreme. Who knew a bunch of soup cans and strands of yarn would get those two to sit still for a few seconds? I owe you one."

"Actually, you owe me two," I said, reminding him of all ten babies of mine he was now in full possession of. You had to remind people these days, or next time you'd see your stuff, it'd be considered a collector's edition.

He led me through the hallway but made a pit stop to a room I almost ignored peeking in when I walked past it the first time in fear that is was someone's bedroom. Looking at it now, with no bed or dressers or anything else that made someone's private chambers personal, it was more a refuge for lounging about. There were all these big cushions on the floor and a massive black wooden cabinet that stood on a riser situated at the center of the north wall. When I didn't follow him inside, he turned to me as he fought the room's closet door open to grab two pillows identical to the ones on the ground.

"Did you want a look inside our altar room?" *So that's what this was.*

I hesitated, being extra cautious with each step I took. There was this collection of expensive-looking vases almost as high as my waist and all these interesting photos hanging up. I didn't want to break anything.

"Felicia, it's okay." He laid the cushions down on the ground. "Nothing's going to happen to you in here. In fact, this is the only place here where you're guaranteed to find peace and quiet. It's not necessary to have a separate room to practice, but my mom is always adamant about having a dedicated spot to do so. There are these unwritten rules that it should be the least active place in the house. You know, to limit distractions?" He pointed to the wooden cabinet and walked me over. "We usually keep this locked when we're not using it, but this is what it looks like inside."

He opened the cabinet's doors' to reveal an interesting layout of items that I was sure held significance, one way or another.

"I changed some of this stuff earlier since my folks were going out. Forced us to practice a little earlier than we normally do. My mom likes it when we're all together."

Along the back wall was a scroll, filled with calligraphy I'm certain Paul couldn't read since his dad knew so little Japanese. On the top shelf, a bronze Buddha statue (or at least I think it was a Buddha) sat regally in the middle along with three candles on the right, left, and in front of the statue. There was also some incense that I'm sure smelled great once it once burned. I didn't want to bombard him with all my curiosity when I knew the real reason I'd dropped by was so we could catch some movie he'd spent the entire night raving about. But he was someone who liked being asked and encouraged questions, even if he didn't know the answer to them. With what time it was, we'd already blown the chance to watch most of the flick, but to me, it hadn't really mattered.

I liked spending time with him. Learning about him and his faith, which he was clearly passionate about. The way his amber-brown eyes moved with measure as he explained the reasons to why every item on the altar had purpose. The way his nose scrunched up when he laughed at my decoration suggestions. And finally, the way his hands, so skilled and unmistakably strong, reached out for mine when he showed me how to hold my hands during a seated meditation. My heart skittered, my knees buckled, and just when my brain mentally registered that it was okay to breathe, I had to remind myself that Paul was actually still trying to have a conversation with me.

"You look like I lost you somewhere. Did you have any more questions?" I did but it wasn't as though it couldn't wait when I saw him next, which with the way we gravitated towards each other would probably be tomorrow. The front door crashed as the sound of Mr. Hiroshima's upbeat whistling traveled throughout the house.

"Hey everyone, we're home!" he yelled from the living room, pretty much meaning this night had come to an unwanted end. "Well, there goes that," Paul laughed. If only he'd known how much I preferred his tutorial over a movie that we could have watched anytime.

"My lamp! What happened to my lamp?!" his dad cried so loud that it was as if he were standing in the room with us. The look Paul gave me told me it was best if I made a quick exit out of there and fast. I didn't know what had happened to his lamp, but the way he spent the next few seconds wailing about it, I wasn't sure I wanted to know.

6
EVEN A HERO HAS A WEAKNESS

FELICIA

"**V**in isit la!"

What did Ma want now? Didn't she know she was interrupting my binge re-watch ritual of Bleach? And when it was getting to the good part!

She yelled for me again as if I weren't moving fast enough for her. I'd made myself comfortable in the basement, formerly Jonasen's room until that loser came back for the holidays. It was the perfect hideaway, a finished basement with everything a girl could want. A comfy fold-out, 24,500 BTU A/C, and an awesome entertainment system that would encourage most people to miss the end of the world. This was a summer bum's paradise!

The further I rushed upstairs, the more fragrant the rich smell of anise stars, vanilla, and cinnamon filled the main floor hallway, a remnant of this morning's Akasan. I wasn't even hungry, but the sweet, lingering scent still made my mouth water the closer I got to the kitchen.

Ma was gossiping on the phone. AGAIN. Geez, what did she want from me this time?

I waved my hands in front of her, but she countered with a held-up finger, beckoning me to wait. All her and Auntie Carol talked about was someone I didn't know or care for. I wanted to ask her in the same way she asks me when she wanted something, "Don't you have something better to do?"

Ma put her palm to the receiver of the phone and croaked in a low voice, "I forgot to tell you. Go next door." I waited for a comment to follow, but nothing. A high-shrieked laugh was all that came afterward, along with an assortment of Kreyol babble. I waved my hands back and forth to get her attention back, but she held up a finger for me to wait as she and Auntie Carol talked about nothing.

"Well, I'm not going to go over for no reason," I made my argument before Ma put her hand on the bottom of the phone receiver and spoke in a low voice.

"I told Robin you would study with her son. She is a teacher. Just bring a book," she said, annoyed that I hadn't followed orders the first time she'd barked them. She waved her hand in the air, shooing me away for good, and I saw that as my way to make a clean break.

I wasn't happy about spending *any* of my August studying. With just three weeks left of summer vacation, I hadn't crossed off more than two of my summer to-do's, and my mother wanted me to spend part of that valuable time next door.

I guess it wasn't *all* bad. It did give me an excuse to go over there. Paul was there. Sure, I didn't want to waste part of my valuable day reading, or whatever it was Ma intended for me to do with a book. But it was my duty as a good daughter to obey my mother's rules, *right*?

I tiptoed to the bookcase in our living room, unsure of what to bring. I assumed when Paul's mom suggested "book", she probably didn't mean comic book. I traced my fingers along the spines facing outward. A few were science fiction and fantasy, more of my dad's personal taste, but very few that weren't my mother's held any profound meaning.

Zoune Chez Sa Ninaine seemed a little too dark to use as study material. A book fell out of place, and when I went to inspect, I tossed it right back. *La Blanche Negresse* was a little too deep for that house. Ma and Daddy needed to buy more than just Haitian authors; there's nothing in English over here!

I noticed one book, *Fille D'Haiti*, and thought about it a little. It was fictional enough not to give someone a lot to think about but educational enough to ensure I wouldn't have to look any further. But in the instance there were less sophisticated choices, I grabbed *Noughts and Crosses* and a few of the new Ms. Marvel comics, just in case.

I played it cool and took my time walking over there. Thirty seconds was long enough, wasn't it?

By the time I reached the porch, my fist was already midway to our neighbor's front door when the garage door opened as Mr. Hiroshima's Toyota Corolla backed out, Kevin and Micah in the back seat.

"Oh, hey Felicia!" Mr. Hiroshima called out. Shoot! I hope Ma hadn't mix up the times. She was so busy on the phone, I didn't think to how long ago that request could've been from, now that I saw Paul's father leaving.

"Where are you guys headed to?" I asked as I brought my hand over to my eyes to block the sun. Mr. Hiroshima held his foot on the brake as he stuck his head out the window to speak.

"Just a little smoothie run. Get the kids out the house." As he lowered his voice to a whisper and held his hand over half his face, like it'd magically make it impossible for anyone but me to hear him. "Just between me and you, though. We're looking for an excuse to bail from Robin and Paul's study time. He can get a little cranky, and the kids being cooped in all day don't help. We were hoping a friend around might make him more comfortable."

I was curious to what he meant by that. They were trying to leave while Paul was supposed to study? What was the big deal? I thought it best not to waste any more time, as Mr. Hiroshima told me it was okay to use their garage door to enter the house since it was already unlocked. As soon as they pulled out the driveway, Micah and Kevin waved until they were no longer visible through the lowered garage door.

I walked through to the door, wandering through a long hallway. I wasn't surprised to hear voices, but I was too much in my own world to notice anything strange about it. All I did was follow where they were coming from. Assuming my mother wanted me home before dinner, I rushed to where the voices were the loudest.

If I had taken my time to the kitchen, I would've heard the constant back and forth. I walked in before I knew what went on, and why Mrs. Hiroshima had asked me to come. "Gosh, mom. I just need a break. I'm trying to get it, but you keep expecting me to move at your pace."

I knocked on the threshold of the kitchen door to announce my presence. It wasn't as if I were expecting a smile or anything, but I definitely hadn't been prepared for Paul's reaction as he pushed his chair away from the table.

"You invited her over here *now*?"

Mrs. Hiroshima threw her arms down in a defeated manner, and already, I'd felt like I walked in on something Paul hadn't meant for me too. "I'm just trying to help you! You seemed to like studying with Beto—"

"Forget it! I'm done anyway," were the last words to leave Paul's mouth before he stood all the way up, more upset than I'd ever seen him. Granted, I hadn't known him for long. This could've very well been the way he was all the time, or at least when I wasn't around. Mrs. Hiroshima made a last effort to get him to stay, but he didn't seem the least bit interested.

"Paul? Paul, come back here—"

"Why? It's bad enough a freaking ten-year-old can do this shit better than me. Now you want Felicia to see? I'll save you the trouble. I can't fucking read!" As all I heard left were the pounding of footsteps and the slamming of a door somewhere in the house. I stood there awkwardly, not sure whether to stay or go as Mrs. Hiroshima turned abruptly toward me and urged me to stay.

"I guess I'll just come by later?"

"No, you can stay. I apologize, Felicia. He wasn't like this back home."

"Did I get the message mixed up? I thought my mother asked me to come over here. But you guys seemed busy." Mrs. Hiroshima gestured me toward the kitchen table as she pulled up a chair close to me, concern wearing heavy on her eyes.

"Did I do something wrong?"

Her green eyes light up, making her appear younger than I assumed she was. "Of course not, Felicia. I think Paul's a little embarrassed. Don't let that outburst fool you. He can, in fact, read; he's just dyslexic and not used to new people knowing." She went on to explain that due to Paul's dyslexia, he was insecure how he sounded reading out loud.

"I told him it's nothing to be ashamed of," she continued on, playing with her nails. "But he's so convinced I push him too hard because I hold him accountable when he doesn't do well. I have experience teaching him outside of a public school, but he's too social for home school. I usually make time to make sure he practices reading out loud, especially so close to the school year." Apparently, from how Mrs. Hiroshima told it, back in Chicago, one, if not both, of his friends, sat in. She said it made him less embarrassed when he had someone besides her helping him.

"I was hoping since you two seem close over the short amount of time that we've been here, that you could push him like his friends did back home. But maybe it was too soon, I don't know." She shrugged off her uncertainty. I wasn't sure what I could do or say, but I guess knowing this much explained the outburst. I didn't know anybody personally with dyslexia, but then again, how would I be able to tell? It's not like you walk around with a label on your forehead or anything.

"I can go talk to him if you want," I suggested before standing up.

She pushed the hair out her eyes and pursed her lips in an unreadable smirk. "I'd rather you not. Paul tends to get in one of his bad moods, and I don't want you to feel slighted by something he does or says when he's embarrassed. Plus, I'd rather him cool off; that way, I can really give it to him for all that swearing," she joked as her faked smile brought out her crow's feet.

I nodded, confirming I understood. "Maybe we can try for another time after I talk to him, okay, Felicia?" Mrs. Hiroshima put her arms around me in exchange for a hug. They must've been a hugging family. Every time I encountered a Hiroshima, it always led to a hug.

I said my goodbyes before heading toward the garage door to go home. At least I'd be home in time for dinner. If I knew my parents well enough, there were legumes in my future, and it always smelled and tasted the best fresh from the stove. I dragged my feet between next door to my house. It never occurred to me how similar the backyards were until someone was living there again.

When I walked into our house, legumes seeped fresh into the air, making my mouth water that it wasn't ready yet. I almost passed the bookshelf but didn't want to bring what didn't already belong in my room all the way for the trip. I hightailed to my door, closed it behind me, and hopped on the bed.

Our blinds were often pulled in, so I don't think Paul knew we could see each other if both of ours were pulled back. But I could see him sitting on his bed, playing on what appeared to be his phone. I'd hoped to get a better look at his space, but he must've felt someone watching him because he turned around like he was trying to avoid me.

That was harsh. It's not like I personally made fun of him or anything, but I suppose he had a right to feel that way. I could wait for another day or approach him head-on and tell him it didn't bother me. I stood near my glass room door to the sides of our houses where our backyards met before I found the courage to slide my door open and walk over to his.

He'd see my shadow if I didn't knock fast, so tapped the glass before I'd look creepy. Paul rolled over to confirm someone'd actually knocked on his glass, got up and unlocked the door, and then sat back down with his back to me. I decided to proceed with caution, shutting the door behind me. "Here to do damage control?"

Based on the bite of that sentence, it was obvious he was still upset about earlier. I calculated what to say, how to say it, or if I should say it at all. Eventually, I decided to hide behind sarcasm, just in case he decided to blow up on me the way he'd done so with his mom earlier.

"I was here to recruit for a covert rescue mission, *but* it's cool if you don't want to go." Paul continued to turn his back to me, on his phone, ignoring me.

"I'm trying to be serious, Felicia," he said with a hint of remorse in his voice. Maybe my attempt at humor wasn't warming the crowd like I'd initially planned, but I wasn't making fun. I was two seconds away from turning around and heading back to my *own* house, but I thought it necessary to mention something before I left.

"I wasn't making fun of you. I didn't even know until like, eight minutes ago. My mother just asked me to come over. I figured, why not, get one thing for something else. I thought it'd be fun to hang out, but now you're mad at me, and I didn't know about it until your mom told me."

Paul sat up for the second time since he opened his door. He gestured toward the comic I still held in my hand, which I couldn't believe I hadn't noticed was still in my hand, as I handed it to him. He flipped to the back of the book where there was an author bio, a paragraph he began to read out loud.

He read each word harshly like he was trying to sound them out for the first time or something, word by word, and one at a time. He sighed of exhaustion when he got toward the end and collapsed his back against his mattress as the comic lay on his side.

"Does that look like I have fun to you?" he asked, devoid of any emotion. I played with a toy Spawn action figure on the dresser closest to his door.

"Okay? But I don't get why you're embarrassed by that. I don't really know anything about it, but it's not like you're like...covered in hives *like Dr. Billman*," I ended in a high-pitched sidekick voice. It could only stand for our arch nemesis, the mailman. Since he brought nothing but bad news, like bill notices, it seemed appropriate.

It was the first time today a hint of a smile crept its way onto Paul's lips. He took the comic, put it over his face, as a muffled groan was all I heard underneath. "Urgh! I just don't want you to think I'm stupid."

My feet were feeling the burn of what it felt like to stand for five minutes in the wrong shoes. I took refuge on a bar stool in front of a canvas in his room. "Why would I think you're stupid? I mean, I'm your friend. Or at least I think I am." I waited for him to take the comic from his face, but he just sat there, idle enough not to know a live body from a corpse.

"Your mom mentioned some of your friends used to help you. Maybe I could help too? If you want!" I offered, with my hands defensively in front of me.

Paul moved his hands, gesturing with his hands toward the ceiling. "Can we like, just save this for another day? All this talk about my weaknesses only make my head hurt."

I offered a small shrug, even though he wasn't looking. I edged back toward the glass door that spilled from my back-yard to his before I remembered I was leaving my comic be-hind. It's not like I didn't trust him, but it was a signed first edition. That needed to leave with me.

I grabbed the comic off his face when he took the opportunity to reach out for my wrist. Hiding behind a smirk, he jerked himself off the bed, wrapping his arms around me. Body parts that weren't tingly were all of a sudden tingly.

"Your parents aren't cooking legume tonight are they?" He must've been psychic, with his 8th Wonder abilities. Either that or he smelled the trace of it in my clothes.

"I don't know. But I'm sure if you asked them nicely…" I don't know what Paul did, but he always smelled really good. I wasn't able to shake him with each step I made toward his glass door, but Paul's bear hug made me feel some kind of way.

"I should probably eat dad's crappy quiche. We don't like to waste food anyway." Paul finally let go and sat at the foot of his bed.

"But maybe if you're not busy tomorrow. I don't know…" Paul trailed off, even though I knew what he meant.

"Okay?"

"Okay."

I walked backward toward the door and let myself out, skipping back to my house. There were worse ways to spend a summer.

7

FIRSTS

FELICIA

My family wasn't big on birthdays. Every year I could remember, I could count on a late Happy Birthday if I heard it at all. Last year was my most memorable. I'd gotten an envelope of cash from almost every relative I had for turning fifteen, but I knew this year would be quieter with my older brother gone for the summer. He was the only one who understood the significance birthdays had meant to me because they had meant a lot to him too. But this year...I hadn't planned on leaving this bed all day.

A series of giggles accompanied by two bouncing bodies was making sure that whatever I *thought* I was going to do today would *not* be going as planned. I pulled the blanket from over my head, relieved to see it was only Micah and Kevin minus the oldest Hiroshima. I'm pretty sure my mom had let them in, but I would have been horrified if Paul saw me in my bonnet and My Little Pony pajamas. Thank God he'd be at work until the mid-afternoon. It was going to take all morning for me to feel fully awake now that I had had unexpected company.

"Hey guys," I squeaked. As much as I would've loved to be left alone, there was no escape from the wrath of the younger Hiroshimas' cuteness. I adored Micah and Kevin, and for some odd reason, they adored me. I was the older sibling Micah always wanted, and she never let a day go by without pleading with my parents to host a trade-in for me and Paul. When my dad found out that Paul could teach him how to break down some of Usher's choreography, he was considering it more and more with each passing day.

My eyes averted to the door when my mom walked in with something I wasn't expecting to see in her hand, not even with it being her day off. Sixteen tiny flames danced along the wicks of sixteen candles, home to a rectangular-sized chocolate cake.

As she brought it closer, the three of them sang the familiar tune of Happy Birthday, in English first, next in French. Although from Micah and Kevin, it was more like mumbling. Someone hadn't gotten enough practice beforehand.

I couldn't help it. I squealed as I blew out the candles. Not only was I getting a cake but on my *actual* birthday. This was more than enough reason to get up and start the day early.

"What kind of cake is this, Ma?"

"Eh, the little one's father made it. I believe it is Devil's chocolate, vegan-style. I wanted to make sure someone would help you eat it, so when I saw the kids playing outside, I invited them over." She sat down on the end of my bed. "I'm unsure of how it will taste. You can be the guinea pig." Micah crawled up to me at the head of the bed, offering to take it downstairs to call dibs on the first piece.

"It's good," she smiled. If she hadn't had darker eyes, she would have looked exactly like Paul. Even me and my brother didn't look that much alike. She cupped her hand over my ear and whispered something that being around their house all the time hadn't struck me as a secret.

"I'd only be worried if my mom helped. Dad is better with the sweet stuff." Well, that was good to know.

Her younger brother followed her downstairs, cake in hand, as I centered my attention back to my mom, who was unknowingly cutting off my circulation by sitting on my feet.

"This is for you." She pulled a box from the floor that I hadn't noticed and probably wouldn't have if I hadn't been woken up early. The package was decently sized and heavy for whatever its contents were. Impatience getting the best of me, I tore the wrapping paper that trapped it, letting the scraps fall to the side of me as my secret gift was finally revealed. It was a black makeup box, with every fold compartment, every slide out tray hosting an article of various sorts of cosmetics.

For two years, I'd begged my mom to let me wear eyeliner and lip-gloss, but she'd always told me that nail polish was the only thing allowed. All the other things were for old people like her.

Why do you want to wear makeup? she'd ask.

You are young; you do not need it, she'd continue.

It wasn't makeup as a whole I liked, but as far as I could remember back, Ma had always worn some form of red lipstick, and she always managed to look beautiful without effort. If I could convey just a sliver of what glam-painted lips had the power of doing for my mom, then all in life would magically come together. "Thanks, Ma." My arms wrapped around her in a bear hug.

"Although I bought an assortment of colors to play with, try to start out with something tame. Like brown or pink. This purple," she held up a tube of dark plum lipstick, "it will age you. Red, you should save for special occasions. Maybe your birthday counts as a special occasion. Enjoy your gift, dear. Don't forget the makeup wipes. It makes getting it off so much easier. Let me go check up on the kids." She made her way to the hallway, and the second I was sure she'd made it all the way downstairs, I rushed to my dresser's mirror, anxious to try out all the new colors on my once bare lips. Now that I'd gotten old enough to experiment, I had a feeling lipstick was going to be my go-to accessory.

Color just sat there. What was I expecting? For me to suddenly look eighteen? I'd filled my lips in with a multitude of shades. Two reds, one true and one burgundy, a vampy purple, which made me look gothic, and three equally similar pinks that hadn't convinced me that either was *the* one. I don't know how my mom did it. She made lipstick look so painless. For me, I didn't look any more mature, any prettier, or any of the other things I noticed when other girls my age boldly wore it. Even with my hair styled in a way that took all night to prepare for, the color on my lips just...sat there. This was going to take some time to get used to.

"Felicia!" my mom screamed from downstairs. I'd literally talked to her five minutes ago. What could be so important now that couldn't be said five minutes ago?

"Felicia!" she yelled again. Only this time, she'd thrown in a few curse words in Kreyol, and she sounded as close as the bottom of the stairs. If I didn't come down soon, she was going to come up here and drag me down.

I examined one last tube that I kept skipping over in fear that it would look too matchy to the fruit punch-like color of the summer shorts I'd put on today. In a rush, I made a clean swipe across my lips with it, and to my surprise, it served its purpose. It made me look pretty.

"Coming, Ma." I got up, dragging my feet all the way down the steps. At the end of the banister, Paul surprised me with a plate in his hand, topped with my birthday cake from earlier.

"Happy Birthday!" he said with his mouth full of chocolate and chewy moist centers. He looked too dressed up to be coming straight from work, and his undercut looked freshly cut and styled as he wore it swept to the side. I took my time making it to the bottom of the staircase until finally, I was face-to-face with Paul. "Sorry, I couldn't have swung by earlier when your mom was cutting the cake. I told Micah and Kevin to wait for me, but I just knew they weren't going to." It was okay, though. Never had I imagined my date of birth to be half as eventful as it was so far. Ever since I was young, my mom never cared about birthdays, blaming the fact that all her siblings had all celebrated theirs on the same day because they weren't as fortunate. In turn, my dad didn't see the point of celebrating them either since according to him, my brother and I had always gotten all we wanted year-round anyways—so, I usually spent my birthday riding around on my bike if it was a nice day out.

Sometimes, if the Phillips were home for the year, Mrs. Phillips would make me these red velvet cupcakes with cream cheese frosting and sprinkles of dark chocolate shavings. But that was only if they were around. Paul's dad's cake was pretty good, though.

"Tell your dad thanks for the cake." Mr. Hiroshima was almost identical to my dad when it came to his kitchen skills. Sure, his entrees were always mouthwatering, but it was his desserts that reigned supreme. My father took pride in mastering the only foods we shouldn't have been allowed to have.

We pulled up two seats at the table, the brass orchestra that accompanied my mother's old school Konpa CDs filled the kitchens airwaves as she got a head start on marinating whatever it was she had planned to make for dinner. If my mom got really into her music, she often forgot when others were around, and when that happened, she danced to her heart's content. It wasn't as though she was a bad dancer. In fact, she was really good, but when the lyrics got too emotional, she always forced the hands of the next available dancer and quite often that someone was always me.

Haitian Konpa should've been simple. From the outside looking in, it looked easy. With its unpretentious steps, I should've been a pro at dancing, but every time my mom had tried to teach me, it was like I had two left feet.

"Ma, stop!" I whined. Paul, who was still sitting down enjoying his cake, had a ball watching me making a fool of myself while I tried to keep up with my mother's foreign dance steps. When she got fed up with my lack of effort, she cast me off to the side and Merengued her way in Paul's direction. He took her hand, and in a few short seconds of aligning his movements to match hers, he'd already learned how to dance like a native of Haiti better than I ever could. *Such a show-off.*

As the song faded into the next track listing, Ma pulled Paul in for a tight embrace, congratulating him on his smooth moves.

"Eh, you are such a good dancer. This one right here could learn a thing or two from you about rhythm," she said, like I wasn't even in the room.

"*This one right here could learn a thing or two from you about rhythm,*" I mumbled to myself in a mocking tone. Because being good at almost everything else clearly wasn't good enough.

"Thank you, Mrs. Abelard. I'm sure my folks told you I danced a lot when I was back home. Hip-hop mostly, but I dabbled in some other stuff, too."

And what other stuff might that be? Being a butt kisser? What was this? America's Got Talent? I was trying to give Paul the courtesy of finishing his cake, but now was the time to get out of this house for the day.

"That's enough outshining I can take for one day. Ma, we're going to go now. I'll try to be back before dinner." At that, she swatted me away like a pesky fly getting on her nerves.

"Oh, don't try to be here on the dot. I only worry when it's you alone. When you're with Paul, I always feel better knowing he's around looking out for you. Paul, don't go getting a girlfriend when school starts and leave poor Felicia to fend for herself," she teased. He laughed leaning on the counter closest to her.

"What if Felicia is the one who gets a boyfriend when school starts and stops hanging out with me. I'm the new one, remember?" he beamed.

"That would never happen. Because she knows she's not allowed to date, don't you Felicia?" I rolled my eyes, knowing that if I argued in front of company, I could cancel going out. Dating was one of those things I didn't question, being an Abelard. My mom freaked out if she thought for one second that I was even looking at a boy, which she would've noticed more often from me if Paul hadn't lived next door. She knew him, she knew his parents, so she didn't think of Paul as the slick boys she thought I went to school with.

He attended temple with his parents without complaint (and liked to). He helped out around his house and had a job, something she desperately tried pushing my brother into getting, every attempt being unsuccessful. In Ma's eyes, Paul was like the poster boy for a child on their best behavior. And for that, my crush on Paul would be just that, a crush.

Not that I'd had a chance with him anyways. I'd gotten a taste for the kind of girls he hung around before he moved here, and they were all hip, city dancer types. Girls who stayed on top of the trends and delivered the latest lingo. I was just a girl from Portland, Maine who was "no-town" instead of "downtown." Hell, half the music Paul listened to, I had never even heard of. I wouldn't come out and say we were complete opposites, but I wondered if anything would change between us once school started in a few weeks, and I wouldn't be his only option when it came to friends.

"How about you, Paul? How do your parents feel about you dating?" He shrugged.

"They're okay with it, I guess. We talk about that sort of thing all the time, and I've only ever had one girlfriend. But they know I'm not really in a rush to do whatever everyone else is doing. I like being invested in someone before I ask a girl out. There's always this pressure to, I don't know, hook up all the time, but my folks always taught me to do stuff on my own timetables. I've got my whole life to be in love, so if I'm not ready, just find other things that make me happy."

Ma nodded as if he'd just recited the deepest of sonnets. *Suck up.* "Your parents are right. This is what I keep telling Felicia. She wants to be, how you say, Yon vyewo li ye wi…"

"I want to be a know-it-all," I offered in English.

"She wants to wear makeup, running in line to be a granmé."

"Gramma," I translated. I pulled Paul towards the door before my mom broke down an entire lesson in Kreyol.

"Ma, see you later. We're going to go now, bye!" I yelled out in one breath. As we reached my front porch, I couldn't help rolling my eyes in disgust at how obedient Paul had been in front of my mother. Saying all the right things and re-enforcing all these expectations that were already set in place for me. I guess that's what happened when you had parents that let you get away with anything. You never had the real desire to break any rules when there were none to begin with.

"What?" he laughed.

"Ugh! Nothing. Let's just get going, okay?" I started towards the sidewalk, but he had other plans in mind.

"Felicia, we've been walking around all week, and it's a hundred degrees outside. Can we please take my car today?" For the show he put on for my mom, I had half a mind to tell him, no, but even I couldn't deny that it was hot out. The petty police were just going to wait until it cooled down some.

When we arrived at the Unforgettable Spot, I'd discovered why he was so eager to get me in his car. It was where he was storing my birthday present, which he refused to give to me until we were outside, seated on the patio steps out back. We'd only met over the summer but had gotten to know each other so well in a few months' time. I was anxious to see what sort of gift he'd had in store for me. I knew patience was a virtue, but right now I wasn't interested in being virtuous. I wanted my present!

"Really, Paul. You didn't have to get me anything," I said, thrilled that he did anyways. The gift was small, flat, and was weightless in my hand, so I had a hard time determining what it could be. Even when I stuck my hand inside the paper he'd wrapped it in—a simple brown wrapping paper he'd adorned with signature doodles—the smooth fabric that caressed my fingertips still left me baffled. I'd have to pull it out to see.

Once in my palms, it took a few seconds to see that it was an eye mask. A superhero eye mask. It was a bright teal that was greener than it was blue, a striking contrast to my pink shorts and white top.

"I don't know how to sew, so my mom helped me with the stitching of the S's on the sides. Other than that, I made it myself. And look…" He pulled out a similar one in purple out of his jean pocket, pulling it over his head and adjusting it around his eyes.

It was official. We were the corniest duo to ever step foot on the planet, but seeing as how his present was handmade, I couldn't help but find it incredibly sweet. Money in an envelope always went a long way, but it was the handmade gifts that made you feel all warm inside. Or least, that's what I had found out today. This was the first time I'd ever gotten a handcrafted gift, but there wasn't anything I'd gotten that made me feel more special.

Just as I'd thought of the perfect words to verbally thank him, I'd done the worst thing that could happen on impulse. I leaned in, and with my heart leading the way, I kissed him.

Paul didn't share the same fullness my lips had, but I'd always admired how right they were for the shape of his face. Getting the up close and personal tour, I had no doubts in my mind on how incredible they'd felt paired with mine. There was a cadence to the way he kissed me that could fool me into thinking that kissing was always meant to be this perfect, but as the sun died down, so did all the feelings I had to go with it. I couldn't be kissing him. I shouldn't be kissing him. The moment the idea traveled to my brain, I jumped back and stood up without hesitation.

With lipstick smeared all along his mouth, he opened his eyes, mystification laced in his expression. From what, I didn't know. Maybe me kissing him?

"Wait! What's wrong? Did I do something wrong?" My face strained from my over analyzation of how bad this was. Why wasn't he freaking out?

"We were kissing! We can't be kissing. This was..." For a reason unbeknownst to me, I couldn't form the proper sentence to articulate my frustration. The only thing I could verbalize was the truth.

"This was a mistake, Paul," I said as I forked my fingers through my thick, once-defined coils. I'd spent all morning experimenting with this new hair style, and already my fingers had their way in destroying it.

"This was a big no-no. It doesn't matter how cute you are or how much I like you," I blurted out before I realized what I was saying. "This all could get me in a lot of trouble. What was I thinking?" I stopped from pacing to look in his direction. "Why didn't you stop me?"

He stood up, and as he rubbed the area surrounding his mouth away with lipstick, it dawned on me that, I too, must have looked like a very sad clown. If only I'd thought to carry makeup wipes.

"I don't know. I guess because I like you, too. Kissing you is really nice," he blushed. "I was so sure that you and I just got along because we like a lot of the same things, but to hear that you like me too makes me feel, I don't know, a whole lot better," he said, releasing a sigh of relief.

"I sort of thought my feelings were one-sided, and I've wanted to ask you out from that day I met you at the tag sale, but I wasn't sure I'd see you again. Then we moved in next door and…"

Without him finishing, I already knew what he was getting at. He'd moved in next door to me, and things were bound to get awkward; although, at this point, we'd skipped past the 'bound'. We were already there.

"Look, I know your mom, and possibly your dad, have a serious issue with letting you date, but we don't have to be in a rush to call it that. I'm usually open with my parents, so they're going to sense something's up with me if I don't tell them. And of course, things might shift a little once they know that, you know, that we like each other as more than just friends."

Before I used to think that there wasn't anything that could make Paul fluster like the way he had when I'd learned of his dyslexia. That was valid. Admitting that you struggled with things that came naturally to another person wasn't the easiest thing to admit, but hearing him talk about his feelings for someone—his feelings for me—was a new type of vulnerability. One that I couldn't even relish in. While we shared the same sentiment, there was nothing to tell his parents because this thing between us was never going to happen.

"Umm…did you not hear my mom earlier? The only reason she trusts us together is because she thinks of us as just friends. To her, you're not like the other boys—"

"That's because I'm not, Felicia," he cut me off. "That's not to say that I'm perfect, but I try to treat people the way I want to be treated. Your mom knows that much about me." I sighed. "Now she does. But if she thought something was happening between us, with a snap of a finger, you'd become one of those *other* boys. And it's not about me being her daughter. I saw it tenfold with my brother, Jonasen, and he's a guy. She didn't like him dating either, and they fought tooth and nail over it. She nearly threatened to send him away when she found out he'd started.

"So what? Am I supposed to forget that you kissed me?"

"Don't forget that you kissed me back!" I snapped. The nerve of him. As if I was the only one to blame in this matter.

"Because I like you. But I also like being your friend." He let out one deep, heavy sigh. "I don't want the relationship we have to change if it isn't what you want. It isn't what you want, right?" he asked with a glimmer of hope in his gaze that was almost pleading.

With his eyes fixed on me, the pressure of saying yes wasn't exactly easy. In truth, it wasn't what I wanted. Paul was my friend, and secretly I'd dreamed of him being into me as much as I was into him. This wasn't how things worked. Best friends didn't fall for each other and when they did, it always took some life-changing moment for the guy to wake up and see that the girl who was meant for him was the one who'd always been by his side.

Paul was bulldozing past all the steps, and now I wasn't ready to accept our mutual feelings for one another. Why couldn't things just happen the way they did in the movies?

"It's what I want, Paul." But judging by the look he gave me, he hadn't read it as the truth. His lips pressed into a straight line as his hands found their way to the bottom of his jean pockets.

"Okay, it's cool. I'll forget it ever happened," he said, accepting defeat as he made a beeline towards the cabin. If he was able to do so, he was better than I was. As much as I wanted to lock it up in the far back of my mind, it was my first kiss. No one ever forgot their first kiss.

8

DEERING'S WELCOME COMMITTEE

FELICIA

Ugh! I couldn't think of anything I dreaded more than the first day of school. Sure, I was a junior now and only one year away from being rid of this place, but still; if there were a way to convince my folks to start school on the second day of school, I would've already figured it out by now.

I decided on a dark floral fit and flare dress my mom bought me a few weeks back when we went back to school shopping, despite her criticizing how manly my legs looked in it. That's what three years of playing soccer will do to your build, but hey, I liked my muscular thighs. Besides, whenever my mom criticized my appearance, it was just her own unique way of saying I looked cute.

"Felicia," my dad yelled before knocking on my bedroom door. "Girl, don't you hear me calling you?" It's official. My dad thinks I'm a basket case. There's no way he'd called my name more than once.

"Come in, Daddy." He peeked his head inside and gave me one of his looks that told me that a cardigan better be going over this dress. I stomped over to the closet and pulled out a slim fit white one as his eyes softened with approval.

"I was just coming up to tell you that Paul's downstairs, offering to give you a ride. Look at you in here, dragging your feet. Don't even have your shoes on. Fè vit! He's not going to wait for long," he said before slamming the door behind him. I hated when he did that.

I took my phone out the charger to send a text Paul's way. *Don't need a ride. Usually walk.*

Before I could throw my phone in my book bag, he texted with a quick reply.

The 8ᵗʰ Wonder needs you. Otherwise, I meet my doom with The Shapeshifter and The Prodigy. Don't make me tackle this mission alone.

Well, when he put it that way, how could I say no? Side-kick Supreme to the rescue.

I gathered all my things and walked downstairs and then outside. Paul was already in his car in what looked like a long, drawn-out battle royal. It made me glad I wasn't the oldest in my family, but still left me curious. Was I that bad to my brother when we were growing up?

"Kevin! I told you not to bring that in here, and what do you do? You spill it all over the floor! What is the matter with you?" he said, angrily. I'd seen him mad before, but some-times I thought he was too hard on his younger siblings.

"Chill out, Paul. It's not like he meant it, geez!" Micah jumped in. I didn't know what the big deal was. There may have been a spot or two that landed on the carpet, underneath the cup holders, but other than that, most of the spill had been caught by the floor covers Paul had.

All it'd take was a quick toss and hose rinse and the covers would look as good as new. I helped Kevin out of the car, and together we walked to the side of Paul's house to find the hose.

"Thanks, Felicia. I don't know why Paul has to be so mean all the time," he said as tears formed at his eyes. I pulled him in for a hug and stroked my fingers through his smooth, floppy hair.

"It's okay, buddy. He's just nervous about school, okay? He knows you're going to make way more friends than he will, and he's just jealous because he knows he's not as cool as you," I said, completely serious.

"Yeah, you're right." he sniffled into my cardigan. I couldn't see how anyone could stay mad at him. He was so sweet and adorable.

"C'mon. Let's finish cleaning this off before Paul makes us walk to school."

"I hate to say it, Felicia, but you just got suckered," Paul laughed after making his final drop off to his sister's school. The car was finally quiet for the first time, although we wouldn't have the silence for long. Deering High was literally in walking distance of the middle school.

Paul looked nice today donning a baseball shirt and slim fit jeans. Crap, what am I doing? I had to stop thinking about my best friend as cute. I told myself it was going to be easy, especially since I'd forced myself to forget he'd ever kissed me just two weeks back. Sometimes, it actually worked.

Once I reminded myself of how much trouble I'd be in or how my parents would limit the time we spent together if they knew that I liked him, it was usually enough to push the thought a blossoming crush to the innermost regions of my mind.

There were the occasional slip-ups. Like when he licked his lips, or when our hands brushed each other's by accident, but typically, this girl had it all under control.

"Yoo-hoo, Felicia," he said as he snapped his fingers I front of my face.

"You okay? I must've asked you four times already, and you were just out of it."

He had this way that he looked at me. A cross between silly and coy and with the faint glow of the way the light looked when the sun hit his brown eyes, maybe even a little mischievous.

Right now, that would be one of those occasional slip-ups.

A part of me feared walking through these hallways with Paul. There was a reason I didn't have many, *correction*, any friends. My freshman year was a tough time for me. I wasn't sure what had made me a target, but I had a run-in with bullying and some girls who convinced themselves that I thought I was better because I performed well, which couldn't have been furthest from the truth.

Trying out for soccer and softball didn't help the situation. It only made it look like I was trying to be better at some of the girls in more than one thing. For a while, I hated going to school. Like, *really* hated it. Until one day, I learned that people only back you into a corner when you let them. The second I started sticking up for myself, the Barbies backed down.

After that, outside of teachers, it was like I didn't exist. I was worse than being unpopular; I was invisible. Anyone who was infected by the disease, otherwise known as Katie Decker, ignored me like the plague. Even the nerds, which hurt the most since we were sort of like brethren. I didn't want Paul to think I was a total loser. Especially since he'd been popular at his other school.

"Hey, what classes do you have?" he asked, breaking my train of thought. I pulled out my schedule as we brought ours up together to compare. Out of four, we had two of the same classes.

"Wow, you're in half all my classes, except for the two you actually placed *higher* than me in. Let me guess; you took those ones last year?"

I cringed, knowing that confirming that I had would make him feel bad. I knew Paul struggled with some subjects, so I didn't want to throw my line of AP classes in his face. Besides, he was artistic. I'd trade brains for that any day.

A few of my former tormentors had given me a few stares, but it could have been because Paul was standing next to me, and it was a sad fact that most people who went here had seen the same people since grade school. A new face?

That was something not even people who hated me could ignore.

The bell went off as students rushed out their seats into the hallway to their next classes. I took a look at my schedule, trying to make out the words that would lead me to my next class.

"Need any help?" A girl popped up next to me, wearing a smile that was miles wide. Her eyes were really pretty, a sort of aquamarine that for a second almost didn't look real against her tan skin. And she was taller than me. Maybe by an inch or two.

"Uhh…just trying to figure out where I should be heading next," I said. "It's fine. I shouldn't have any issue finding it. But what you could do is help me figure out for Room 303, if I have to take a right or left out of here." I backed away towards the door.

"Left," she said as she ran her fingers through her thick, wavy, brown hair.

"My left, or your left?" My last attempt to make a joke.

"Your left," she pointed. I bumped into the wall like a dummy, but at least it wasn't in the face. That would have been hard to recover from.

Her infectious laugh filled my ears, and if I hadn't been in such a rush, I would've gotten her name. I wondered whether everyone that went here was this nice.

It was finally lunch time, and I was grateful that the juniors and seniors lunch block was together. It was tough being at a new at a school I obviously stood out in. It wasn't as if there were no brown people, that wasn't my issue at all. Our first day in Portland, I'd convinced myself that Felicia's family were the only other non-white family in town, but no, I was surprised at how diverse it was. But one of the first conversations Felicia and I had about the kids that went to Deering was maybe, just a little bit true.

Most of the guys looked like they walked out of a pod person factory. It was like there was a specific formula to the way the guys dressed, what they took interest in, and even the way they wore their hair. In a sea full of prepsters, I'd definitely gotten some looks. Wasn't complaining about the way a lot of girls giggled when I had the pleasure of walking by. I definitely felt like I was *really* The 8th Wonder. In case you were wondering, I did say that in my dramatic superhero voice, echo and all.

"Hey."

Felicia caught up to me just as I was headed to the cafeteria. Talk about great timing. As we stood in line for food, I couldn't help feeling impressed with how many vegetarian options the café had available. At my old school, I usually brought my own lunch, but in a rush to get my brother and sister ready, it slipped my mind.

Sweet. They had macaroni and cheese and vegetarian pizza. I was in heaven.

After Felicia did the honors of treating me, I was a bit confused when she pranced away with the tray in her hand in the opposite direction of the lunch room.

"Uhh, what's up, Felicia?" The look of confusion plastered all over my face. "You're going the wrong way."

I stood, tray in hand, in front of her. She went around me and kept on walking.

"Hey Felicia, you sure you've been going to this school for three years? Because it's obvious you don't know where the cafeteria is," I said, joking, but something told me that I probably shouldn't have. Halfway through the halls, Felicia stopped with something unreadable in her expression.

"I don't eat in the cafeteria, okay? I usually eat in the library. You don't have to follow me. I just...I don't like eating around other people. It's hard to explain." Without another word, she stalked off in the library's direction. Guess I knew where I was headed.

I didn't have much time to catch up to Felicia before she ducked into the library. The minute I was outside, I was bombarded by the personification of school spirit. "Paul Hiroshima, right?"

I turned to face the person who'd just called my name but didn't sound the least bit familiar. A furrowed brow and tight jaw was accompanied by an "Um, yeah?" in the stranger's direction. It was a guy around my age, maybe older. He was about six feet, so I couldn't tell if he was a junior or senior. But with a book bag, stack of papers, folders, and a clipboard tucked under his rib, it was obvious he at least attended school here.

"Adrian Sanou. I'm with Deering's welcome committee." As he extended his hand out for me to shake, and so not to look rude, I balanced my tray on my forearm and offered my hand back. "I've been meaning to chat with you earlier, but you didn't seem to need a guide or anything. You're friends with Felicia, right?"

I nodded, still confused on what he wanted since he approached. Seemed like a nice guy. Definitely hadn't stopped smiling since he got my attention. I'd say if there ever were an embodiment of Maine, morphed into a person, this guy had to be it. He was wearing boat shoes for crying out loud. But of the entire day, he'd been the only student to approach me, let alone introduce himself. By my standard, that made him a cool guy.

"Yeah. We're neighbors."

Adrian nodded as if it made perfect sense. "Ah. I know her from around too. Anyway, I just wanted to introduce myself. As part of the welcoming committee and student council, know that if you ever need anything, I'm here to help. Don't be afraid to ask."

"Okay?" I laughed back, not sure of how to take all that friendly in one serving. He tapped me on the shoulder and smiled one last Ken doll smile before he excused himself and let me be on my way. Don't ask me why, but he reminded me of a young River Phoenix, only with brown eyes. Was some-one supposed to look like that in high school?

I'd already wasted five minutes of lunch period trying to catch up to Felicia and with Adrian's introduction, so I didn't waste another one as I raced past the metal detector in the library to find Felicia in the back.

Her body language read *Don't talk to me*, and I knew she'd been upset about something before she walked inside. But I mentally prepared myself for anything that might get thrown my way. I didn't expect her to ignore me altogether. Or rather, not talk at *all*. There wouldn't have been any communication our entire lunch period if I hadn't mustered up the courage to break the awkward silence.

"So, this Sanou kid came up to me. Said he knew you," I offered casually.

Felicia shrugged off the comment and replied back with, "We're not friends or anything. He just goes to my parents' church." Oh! That explained the pep.

"He mentioned being part of student council or some-thing?" I stated and asked at the same time.

"He's the commissioner of spirit. Don't be surprised if he's super annoying leading up to school spirit week," she ended in a light sigh like she wasn't even interested in elabo-rating further.

Whatever was eating at her affected her mood for the re-mainder of the day. She had soccer practice after school, and even though I offered to wait for her, she all but made it clear not to bother. A clear sign she was still upset by something. I didn't intend on making her mood worse, so I ignored the whole situation altogether.

Something told me, that whatever bothered her, would re-veal itself in time.

9

DECISIONS, DECISIONS

FELICIA

I dreaded the early a.m. practices that forced me out of the bed an hour and a half before school. The afternoon slot was slated for the boys' football team, so in favor of the boys, aka the star team, we girls were subject to a time where we were all tired and cranky and just plain fed up with anything sports-related. Maybe it would've been easier to take up basketball. At least the girls' basketball team got to play inside, and the weather never affected whether they played or not. At my house, there was no mention of basketball, and as far as my dad was concerned, we were a soccer-only household. It was no wonder to why by the time I was nine, I was bouncing balls off my head and able to dribble across a field like nobody's business.

I had a love/hate relationship with soccer. I loved playing it but hated my teammates. Perhaps hated was a strong choice of a word. It never changed the fact that, off the soccer field, I went on not existing to most of them. They were a tight-knit bunch of girls who'd gotten everything they wanted and had been friends for years. When Katie Decker got injured during last week's game, her close friends Julia Araújo and Becca Carson were so sure they'd be shoo-ins for her oh-so-coveted position. They were all seniors, so they deserved it, right? That's what I thought, too. Until Coach Del Vecchio made the announcement at the end of practice who'd be replacing her, throwing everyone for a curveball when he called my name instead of one of theirs.

I knew for sure I'd earned it. I'd worked so hard over the summer and last year was so disappointed in myself for not scoring the position I wanted. But this season, I was in top form and yet…A part of me hadn't fully thought about what accepting the change would mean for me.

All the girls gathered as Coach called time on practice. It was seven fifteen, and with school starting, a group of sixteen sweaty girls needed some quality time with soap and running water. I stayed around to talk to Coach to see if I could get him to reconsider his decision. A few of my teammates were already sneering and whispering, one of them even *bumped* into me on her way off the field. If there was something I could do to limit the harassment, there was no better time than now.

"Coach." I approached Coach Del Vecchio as he secured his bag over his shoulder and dumped his car keys in his pocket.

"Congrats on all the hard work, Abelard. These last few games you've been unstoppable— "

"Yeah, that's what I wanted to you talk about," I said clutching my right arm in my left hand. "Are you positive I'm ready to play forward? I don't mind staying where I am for now. At least not until next year when I'm a senior." He rested his hand on my shoulder.

"Abelard, I don't make decisions based on seniority. I reward the players who play with the best spirit. You don't play like a star player. You play like a winner, selfless. And that, in turn, makes you a star player. It was between you and Becca Carson but between me and you, you've got the magic. You've got the grades. You're one of the few girls I worry about on this team. This isn't about your teammates, is it? Because they know we've got a zero tolerance for bullying. Anyone touches you, and they know they're off the team."

Katie Decker and Becca Carson were pretty much evil personified. Just because they couldn't touch me didn't mean they wouldn't find loopholes to get under my skin. They were popular and had tons of friends. It almost didn't seem worth it when I had another year, one where they'd be long gone, to shine.

"Look, if you want the spot, it's yours. If at any time you change your mind, it'd be great to know by the end of the day. Don't, for a second, think that someone handed this to you. You're a great player. Remember that," he trailed off, leaving me with a *lot* to think about. I had until the end of the day to give him my decision, but that meant I also had all day to talk myself out of it.

As I fished through my mangled mess of a locker, two hands firmly gripped the back of my shoulders, causing my heart to leap out of my chest. I shouldn't be freaking out, but I was expecting for something to happen; I just didn't know when it would happen. Maybe luck was on my side today and there was nothing really to worry about. But going off that logic, which only assumed I'd made through the whole day without any mishaps. The clock on my locker's wall read seven fifty. I still had a long way of this day to go.

"How was practice? The sound of Paul's soothing voice calmed my nerves. I was wondering when he'd show up since because of practice, he wasn't able to give me a ride to school this morning. Either way, I was glad it was only him.

"Ehh, it was okay."

"Just okay?" he asked with lifted brows.

"Hey Felicia, congrats on scoring forward today," a voice surprised us from behind. It was Julia Araújo, one of the few girls I actually tolerated on my soccer team. She was friends with Becca and Katie but somehow she'd managed to keep her soul intact. To be friends with them, I couldn't see how you needed one.

"Hi," she said with a perky smile in Paul's direction.

"Hey," Paul replied back yet hadn't returned the same warmness. It was five seconds away from entering awkward territory, so I couldn't say I wasn't thankful when she waved goodbye and made her exit. I knew that Paul had had a certain effect on girls, but to witness it firsthand just made me want to gag on my insides. People acted like they'd never seen a cute boy before and I mean, c'mon, it's been a whole month now. The moment she disappeared out of view, he leaned on the locker beside me, grinning in an annoying but lovable sort of way.

95

"So…when were you going to tell me about the up-grade?"

"Uhh…probably about the same time I told you I planned on turning it down." The confusion wasn't lost in his eyes as they widened and narrowed trying to figure out a fitting way to answer.

"Okay, so you know sports isn't really my thing but isn't a forward like the quarterback of soccer or something? Why would you turn it down?"

"Because it's not important to me where I play. I just like playing." That and I didn't want any trouble from any of the other players. I was patient and only played for fun. A few of my teammates had scholarships riding on playing, whereas, I was lucky enough to not have to worry about that sort of thing. With my performance alone, I could get into any school of my choice, and my mom and dad planned for education like some countries planned for war. I hated the idea of taking away someone's opportunity to be seen, especially since I knew a top university was already in the game plan, whether I played soccer or not.

But still, to hear what my dad might say, knowing I was good enough to make lead scorer, he probably would be so proud of me.

"I don't know, Felicia. It seems silly of you not to accept. Especially if you're good. But hey, what do I know?" As much as I wanted to confide in Paul the real reason I'd be turning the spot down, it had been a peaceful couple of weeks for me. I didn't want to spoil it by getting Paul all worked up and worried when things were finally perfect…at least for now they were.

It was a quarter past twelve, and I was feeling optimistic about going the whole day incident-free. Becca and Katie hardly did anything when their mediator Julia was around, so although Becca Carson had approached me with one of her backhanded compliments as I was heading to my Block Three class, the interaction I'd had with either one of them was tame. Everything was going well until I needed to get something out of my locker before my next class started. The moment I'd gotten a whiff of someone's musky, cedar cologne, I thought I was going to choke on how strong the scent engulfed me. It was the captain of Deering's football team, Duke. I suppose it was too good to be true to think that a few girls would let it go.

Duke Sheridan was one of those pretty boys who would date their own reflection if he was smart enough to figure out how to. He was tall, almost a head taller than Paul, and his eyes were a villainous shade of blue that made looking at him almost painful. I guess he was good-looking if you liked arrogant, narcissistic psychopaths who could make your archenemy look like an ally in the heat of an epic battle. He was actually sort of nice to me my sophomore year when I got stuck tutoring him in Chemistry in order for him to stay on the football team. I even sort of had a crush on him, and for some dumb reason, I thought he had felt the same way—that is—before he started dating Becca Carson.

"Hey, Felicia. What's going on? Haven't talked to in forever."

"You mean you haven't pestered me in forever."

"C'mon, Felicia. Stop being so sensitive. I remember a time when you were actually nice to me."

"Yeah, and I remember a time when you were a decent human being, but it looks like we can't all revert back to the better versions of ourselves. You're just stuck being who you are and me? Well, I'm too busy being sensitive. Now, if you don't mind…"

He slammed my locker's door in an effort to rattle me, but I stood firmly in my stance.

"So, what's this about you robbing Becca out of Forward? You're not exactly thinking about taking it, are you? Because I can't promise it'll turn out well if you do. You know how my girlfriend is with finding her…loopholes. I'd hate to see something bad happen to you on the strength of her being in a less than stellar mood," he shrugged. "You know how she gets."

He attempted to put his arm around me, but I pushed him away, not wanting the awful stench of rotten person left all over me. I didn't know how long it could take to rinse myself free of jerky asshole, but I wasn't willing to find out.

"You could tell your stupid little girlfriend that I'm not going to take it. She can have it if she wants. Just don't touch me." A dose of something sinister flashed on his face, knowing he'd gotten his wish without having to get his hands dirty. I honestly couldn't remember why I ever even liked him. He seriously reminded me of one of those guys who assaults a girl and then throws a party because he got away with it. Another reason why I didn't want his grimy paws on me.

"Glad I could be so persuasive," he said as he drew in closer, too close for my own comfort. He reached out to touch me as I again shoved him away, only to watch Duke get slammed into the locker next to me with Paul being on the other end of the attack.

"Didn't you hear what she just said, tough guy? Hands to yourself." The fire in Paul's eyes brought me back to all the times I witnessed him lose his temper with his siblings, only, this time, he was plain furious.

"Chill out, new kid. Felicia and I were just having a little talk."

"Yeah, well do your talking someplace else," Paul argued. Duke looked at me for confirmation, looking for me to diffuse the hot fuse otherwise known as my best friend.

"Ugh, it's okay Paul. We were just talking. *He* was making sure I knew how miserable his girlfriend would make me if I accepted her beloved position on the soccer team. Don't worry, Duke," I spat. "I got the message loud and clear."

"See, new boy. Relax. No one's going to touch your little girlfriend," Duke said as he nudged Paul a few steps back.

"My name's not 'new boy'," Paul shuffled back after being hit with another one of his light shoves.

"Paul, just walk away. He's not even worth it," I begged before the situation got the opportunity to get worse.

"Dude, I'm telling you. You don't want to mess with me," Paul smirked, clearly annoyed but doing his best to keep the situation neutral. "Is that so?" Duke spat as he once again forced Paul backward. A small crowd formed around us, unable to resist the beginner makings of brawl set to ensue only minutes before our next classes, but if I had any say in it, no said fight ensue. I didn't want Paul to get hurt. Not over this.

"Paul, don't let him get to you. Let's just go."

"Yeah. Listen to your little girlfriend, new boy. Word of advice to you since you're new around here: Don't start something you can't—"

I don't know how I didn't see it coming, but for the first time since approaching me, Paul had gotten Duke to shut up.

He'd managed to land a punch dead center on Duke's once pretty face, filling the hall with his dreadful groan and the sound of Paul's fist cracking against something hard.

"Now, what were you saying about starting something I couldn't finish?"

Duke clutched onto his nose, clenching his jaw and gritting his teeth like a pit bull ready to pounce on what he thought was a defenseless animal. Only Paul was no defenseless animal. He was willing, just as he was clever and getting a kick out of making a fool out of Duke. As Duke struck back, Paul dipped out of the way, leaving his blundering opponent to fall flat on his face.

"Man, if you hit as hard as you take a dive, we might even have a real fight on our hands. Told you that you didn't want to mess with me." But he'd had spoken too soon. Duke rose to his feet and hit Paul with a deadly right hook and just then a lost voice in the flock that surrounded them had yelled "Fight!" making others gather around to see the so-called struggle, and who had started it. For a short second, I thought that one of them was going to be the better man and call it a draw. Both of them were taking a beating and both of them looked ready to tap out, but you know how stupid guys were in their quest for complete dominance. I can't say I wasn't thankful when Duke's girlfriend, Becca and her friends Katie and Julia entered the circle, Julia even being brave enough to put herself in harm's way in attempts to pull Duke off of Paul.

"Duke, what's the matter with you? Becca, Katie, did you have something to do with this?" she asked, looking to her guilt-ridden friends. As if things couldn't get worse, Principal Castillo also took interest in why a mob of his students had gathered around but had trouble finding their way back to class. That's when he noticed Duke and Paul all battered and bruised up as the result of their quarrel. She ordered everyone back their classes but had different instructions for the two boys. Our school had a zero tolerance policy when it came to fighting. I didn't need superpowers to know what punishment lied ahead. It was all my fault.

I perused the familiar hallways of my previous school of attendance, old memories flooding back of the four years I spent here patiently waiting to be old enough to go to Deering. Now that I was there, I couldn't help wishing for simpler times when I didn't have catty rivals, and the highlight of my day was competing in the science fair.

I used to think it was so cool that Lincoln, the middle school, was just an inch away in walking distance to the high school, but now that I was an attendee, all that meant was the same people you spent years avoiding there reserved another four-year slot to contribute to your fear and torture. I was someone who worked hard. I had to if I wanted to try out for teams since my parents put education first and told me recreational hobbies (as my mother called it) would only distract me from keeping my grades up. I'd proven to my mom and dad that I could be good at more than one thing, and I didn't think I was better than anyone because of it. But the problem with people who thought of themselves as entitled, it didn't matter what *you* thought. If they thought for a second you did think you were better, you became a problem.

I wasn't going to let a few girls and their blockhead boy-friends scare me out of a spot that I'd earned. Nope. I was going to accept the position and spend the rest of the season rubbing it in their faces, but now my guilt settled at the base of my stomach, knowing Paul had gotten into it with that Neanderthal defending me. *What the hell was he thinking?*

I heard Micah's bold laugh before I was able to spot her. For a ten-year-old, she had the loudest laugh I'd ever heard. On second thought, the only person who beat her out of that award was her dad. Even at the corniest things, Mr. Hiroshima could out laugh a pack of hyenas. It was actually sort of scary.

I waved my hand to grab Micah's attention and waited while she and that blonde girl who was like her shadow approached me, wondering what was up.

"Hey, umm, Paul is in detention, so if you were trying to go home now, it looks like we'll be walking." Micah's eyes swelled up with delight, demanding every last detail as to why he'd gotten thrown in the big house, but I had no intention of throwing Paul under the bus only so his little sister could have something to hold over him later. As much as I loved Micah, Paul was my accomplice, my sidekick, my partner in crime. If she wanted to hear more of why he was facing punishment, it wasn't going to be from me.

"C'mon, Felicia," she pleaded. "Just one little detail, please! I promise I'll stop asking if you leave me with something. Did he at least get roughed up a little?"

After some thoughtful consideration, I realized for a guy Paul's size, that fight could have gone a number of different ways. While he wasn't short, he didn't have Duke's height or even his football build. And yet, he succeeded in walking away minus Duke Sheridan's black eye and busted lip. Had Paul gotten roughhoused? *Maybe.* But that hadn't meant he'd lost the fight either, especially if it hadn't been broken up.

"Micah, let's go. I already promised your dad I'd have you home after school. Any talking you want to do has to be on the way." Thankfully, she agreed.

On the way home, the thing I'd found weird about her friend, whose name I later learned was Nala, didn't say much. Or maybe it was that Micah talked so much that it was hard to out-talk her. The whole way to the Hiroshima's, they were closed off in their own little world that consisted of fifteen minutes of solely Micah's input with the occasional animated nod from Nala. I hadn't bothered interrupting since I'd had so much on my mind, but I couldn't understand how a whole conversation could be had with just one person talking. Maybe that was normal for them.

We all took our shoes off upon entering their house as Paul's dad rushed from the basement to the living room to uncover the latest update.

"Dad, if you haven't heard, Paul got into a fight at school and totally earned his detention. I'd say that calls for some epic sort of punishment, don't you think?" Mr. Hiroshima's face contorted into an expression that was slightly irritated but still seemed to answer Micah back with a great level of patience.

"Micah, honey, we talked about that. While it's great that you occasionally do exceptional spy work, you shouldn't get any pleasure out of someone else's downfall. Plus, it's only exceptional when you bring me *new* information. There's no point in gloating on facts I *already* know." Her dad turned to me and gestured for me to follow him in another room.

"Mind if I have a word with you alone, Felicia?" Micah crossed her arms, wearing a look of disgust and bitterness, knowing she wouldn't be hearing the whole story in detail like she initially hoped. I didn't want to talk about it either, but I suppose I wouldn't be a good friend if I didn't at least tell his dad that he'd only thrown the first punch to protect me. In essence, the fight wasn't even his fault at all. It was mine.

Before Mr. Hiroshima and I made it into the next room, the phone in his hand rang, sending him in a panic to pick it up. His body language drowned in relief as the moment he got off the phone, he couldn't stop saying, "*Thank you.*"

In a rush, he ran past me to yell for Micah to gather up her things for the night since Nala's mother had extended an invitation for Micah to spend the night at their house. I couldn't help wondering if their dad was always this frantic, or if he were preparing to do away with their eldest son and just didn't want any witnesses around. When he ran back to me, I was still standing in the hallway where he left me as he caught his breathe in search of another favor. He pinched the bridge of his nose.

"Okay, so I wanted to talk to you about the whole Paul thing, but he's going to be home in a little while, so maybe it'll be better if I just hear it from him. I would like one more favor to ask of you, though. If it's okay with your folks."

With what I owed Paul, I don't have the right to say no.

"The girls are sleeping over at the Sanous'. It's just a few blocks over; would you mind walking them? I'm pretty sure they're on Glecker Road, but you can double-check with Nala to make sure." But it turned out I wouldn't have to. I knew enough about the Sanous to know where they lived.

They were the only openly gay couple anyone had known with kids in this neighborhood, not to mention the very unnuclear setup of one of their ex-wives still living there with them. Everyone used to sneer at them, my mom included. But once they started going to my parents' church, and my mom actually got to know them, she became one of their biggest defenders. Even when they weren't around to hear it.

My mom was conservative in most areas, but judging people on who they'd decided to love was the one topic she was easily swayed over, especially when they shared the same faith. She loved the Sanous and due to the constant potlucks their church always held, they loved her right back.

They were always trading recipes, and I think she even asked for their advice on how to be more welcoming when my brother came out as bisexual. Because of this, I'd waited in the car outside their home on several occasions while my mother promised to only be one minute. Sure, I knew where they lived. As well as escape routes, hiding places, and even what time their mail usually came. That's how many times I'd been outside their house.

"Oh, and if you didn't know, Nala is insanely shy. She barely talks to anyone. Don't take offense if she doesn't talk. It took her until last week to warm up to me. I know it isn't a long walk or anything; it's just, I thought you should know if you haven't gathered that already."

He took in a deep breath and headed for his bedroom. "Felicia, promise me one thing! Never become a parent. And if you so happen not to follow my advice, stop after the first kid. The rest, they're just too hard to keep track of," he said as a joke but given the situation of today's news with his eldest, I had a feeling he sincerely meant it.

"Go on," Micah nudged her friend Nala to answer my last question. "She's actually really nice. Not annoying like my older brother," she whispered. It was almost impossible to spend the entire way to her house, listening to Micah babble on about topics that even when I was their age, bored me to death to listen to it then.

Put me in a room filled with RPG's, and you could count on me not leaving the room until an important event was slated to happen. Apparently, the two of them felt the same way.

"I don't know; I guess I sort of like that new Phoenix Festa game, but ever since I broke my PS Vita, my brother refuses to let me play it on his PS4. So I never got to finish it to the end. I like to, but I don't play as much as Micah. She has almost every console ever made, but I only had just the one," Nala replied. She had one of those deep, mature voices for her age that threw me for a curve when I'd finally heard her speak. It didn't match her appearance but still, she was only eleven. Maybe the rest of her development was bound to catch up sooner or later. She was insanely sweet, though. Once she'd warmed up to me, I found out the hard way that she was just as talkative as Micah, maybe even more. Relief set in when the sight of her porch finally came into view.

"Hi, Felicia!" Nala's stepfather greeted me at the door as he led me through the kitchen to offer me a cup of licorice and honey tea he'd finished brewing. Inside, I'd passed Nala's birth father on the couch where he was watching TV. I was surprised to see Adrian from school pulling out a tray of something that smelled of warm, melting chocolate just ready to be demolished. I didn't want to seem rude, so while I wanted one, I was hoping someone would just offer. I wasn't a tea person, but I was definitely a brownie person.

He jumped back shocked to see me, which only made me feel like I had something in my teeth. Either that or he was one of those people who hated running into people from school. *Well, that made two of us.*

"Hey, Felicia," he managed to say as his cheeks burned a light crimson. "I heard what happened at school. I hope they don't hold Paul to the same standard as Duke. He's always trying to intimidate people; I'm just glad someone finally stood up to the guy. Sorry that it had to be your friend, though. I hope they don't suspend him." Before I could open up my mouth to respond, in came Micah and Nala rushing into the kitchen, begging if I could spend the night with them in what appeared to be, not including the two of them, a sleepover for three, and I wasn't trying to be the fourth. A girl's night with a bunch of ten and eleven-year-olds didn't sound like any way to end the night. Plus, I wanted to see how Paul was holding up. That, and to uncover any remains that his parents may or may not have left behind.

"Sorry, guys. I'm pretty sure my parents want me home tonight but maybe next time, okay?" On my way out, the dad who had been sitting on the couch had gotten up to walk me to the front door and wished me goodbye. And to find out what my mom and dad were bringing to their church's fundraiser this weekend. Adrian materialized on the porch the second I'd made it to the sidewalk and also waved me goodbye. Was it weird that when he wasn't in school and getting on everyone's nerves that he was actually sort of cute? Maybe his eyes didn't gleam like Paul's did. And his style was like all the boys I'd known growing up, so he blended in instead of standing out like Paul had. But his dreamy, wavy brown hair always seemed to fall over his eyes in an intentional way even though I know he probably just didn't get regular haircuts, so it was most likely a coincidence. Still…*cute*.

My cell phone buzzed with two messages from my mom wondering how far I was from home. Rather than text her right back, I decided it best to put my legs through a workout and power walk the way home before my mom sent out a search crew. It was only four thirty, and Paul was due home soon. I didn't know what he was facing, but the least I could do was bring him his missed assignments from school.

10

A "PAUL" A

PAUL

Just in case you were wondering, sitting in detention with a bunch of fake people you were forced to be around was most likely *not* the way to keep positive vibes in a messed up situation. I should've kept my temper at bay, but something just snapped in me.

It took a real loser to intimidate a girl so much smaller than you. I wasn't going to just sit there and watch some jerk scare Felicia into thinking she had to do what they told her. For her sake, I hope she did what was best for her and not let them bully her into making a decision. Unfortunately, I wouldn't even know until I got home later, and that's only as-suming I survived tonight.

I wanted so bad to shoot this so-called Duke Sheridan in-timidating stares. It wasn't every day you got your ass handed to you, and from our first encounter, Duke knew not to start anything involving Felicia or me. But I knew after today, it'd be my last fight. Mom was going to kill me.

I thought I'd have more time to consider what I was going to say to her once I got home. I'm sure the school secretary blabbed on me, and if not them, Micah and Kevin. I couldn't trust Felicia not to be manipulated by their powers of the mind, and she'd convince herself the sidekick in her couldn't hold out. But neither of that mattered because the minute I stepped out the library where detention was held, that sense of security was stripped clean from my mind.

"Paul. You are in A LOT of trouble."

Never mind that I was her first born child. Never mind that Mom knew me well enough to know there was no way I could've started this. Never mind that I was defending a friend. All Mom heard what that I'd gotten into a fight. And for that, I had to deal with her ominous disappointment.

She'd walked to Deering, with the intention of beating me to my car, so she could drive me home. We'd had sets of mul-tiple keys of everything, just in case I lost mine; it meant there'd always be a spare at home. I hated the idea that my parents could hijack my car anytime they wanted when I didn't have the same privilege with theirs, but Dad always prided himself on never being seen in my driver's seat.

"Aren't we off to a good impression," Mom said, her voice cold and passive. Sometimes it was what Mom *didn't* say, over what she actually did. She'd made it known that this school year was my last one to shape up. Education should've been my first priority, but we both knew that was code for *hers*.

When I couldn't find the words to answer her that wouldn't get me in more trouble, she broke the ambiance of the car, once again. "Well, I'm sure you'll have more to say once I take your car privileges away for two weeks— "

"Mom, seriously?"

"Oh, now he speaks."

"Are you even going to ask me what happened?" I asked without thinking.

"I'm not sure I care at this point. I know the move's been hard on you, but seriously, Paul. It's time you got your fucking act together," she said under an irritated huff. My parents weren't one to swear for no reason. Dad had a few triggers. One being cut off on the freeway. Another being when he stubbed his toe or walked into a wall. Then there's when on the occasion he did drink and had one too many…

But Mom? She swore when she was mad. I mean, boiling point mad. And it was supposed to be our little secret when she swore like a sailor when Dad wasn't around. Typical of a hypocrite. Do as I say, not as I do, especially when it was something she didn't want Dad knowing about. When she picked up her phone to text, I just knew that whatever she was texting had to be a bat call to Dad.

"Don't crash on the way home." I made sure to sneer under my breath. But the Dictator *heard* everything. She was probably straining her super sonic hearing just to see if I'd huffed with an attitude or something.

"I'm sure you'd like that. But I was just texting your father about how much of a smart ass you're being. He's always trying to play good cop, and that's not what you need right now. So, I want him to know *everything* up until the time we pull up in that driveway."

Of course, she was just mad she always had to play bad cop. My Dad understood me in a way she couldn't. She'd always pressured me to work harder, do better. She didn't always see that I *was* working hard and trying to do better. It wasn't as if I didn't want to attend a university. Or college should the cost be an issue. I just couldn't help that we had different definitions of what was better.

Dad could be hard on me too, but most times he chose not to be. He tried to understand me in ways Mom wasn't able to, and even though he didn't always take my side, the fact he was willing to *see* my side meant a lot to me.

I had high hopes to attend a school that'd actually nurture my talents, not discard them. Mom loved my ability to create, but in more ways than one, she'd made it clear that art was a hobby and that I needed something reliable to fall back on.

In high school, nothing sounded reliable to me. But it was convenient how all the things I excelled at were all the activities my mom would deem as "hobbies." I would've loved considering the idea of art school, but I knew there was no chance my parents would ever let me. So, I was forced to anticipate what the silence meant, up until Mom pulled up to our sidewalk.

I swear the car ride home was as uncomfortable as Mom could make it, without raising her voice. The Dictator was good. She didn't require much more than to exist when it came to inducing fear.

"I guess I'm sorry I got in a fight. But I'm not sorry *why* I got in a fight." After I said it, I knew it hadn't been the best move.

The house was still and quiet as we'd walked through the front door. Much quieter than I expected. Aside from Kevin exhausting his television privileges for the week, the only other commotion came from the kitchen. Dad had to be starting dinner or at least putting the finishing touches.

"Where are Nala and Micah?" Mom asked, leading the way into the kitchen.

Dad turned to face her, licking the remnant of whatever was on his fingers from the sauce he'd prepared for what looked like spaghetti squash pasta. "Yeah...I figured the least of our problems right now might be more kids around the house. When Nala's parents called, inviting them to a sleepover, it just seemed like the best idea."

That or Dad foreshadowed a long, drawn out argument about my future in this house. Mom had made it clear what privileges I'd lose as far as she was concerned, but didn't seem satisfied that I'd been punished enough. And she wanted Dad to back her up on it.

At least Micah wasn't here. She'd probably be waiting on the staircase, listening in, just so she could rub it in my face later. I'm sure for the right price, Kevin would dish everything he could get his ears on from the living room without seeming obvious. But with Mom on my case, and her desperate attempt to get Dad on her side, my siblings should've been the least of my problems.

I'd sat at the table for a few seconds before Mom and Dad decided to join me. I already knew Mom was going for severe punishment, but Dad was much harder to read. He hid behind a passive look in his eyes, accompanied by a small frown. "So what happened?" he finally asked, eager to get the ball rolling before dinner.

I took what felt like the deepest, longest breath I'd ever taken and replied as emotionless as possible. "I got into a fight. There's not much else to tell."

Mom's eyes widened, like she was expecting a more smart-ass answer, but looked over to Dad to study his expression.

"Okay Paul, you don't have to get cute. I'm not taking sides or judging here. I just want to know what would cause you to put yourself in a situation like that. That's not like you. I really want to understand."

Even though it'd been the third time I had to explain things, by the time I got to Dad, it'd been a much calmer version of what was standing up for a friend. Both my parents didn't condone fighting, but they didn't encourage it either. In their opinion, unless your life was in eminent danger, most situations could be diffused with words.

"I see," Dad added, before tapping the table with his fingers. "Well, Paul. I can't defend you 100%. My opinion on fighting still stands that it wasn't the answer in this situation. But since your mother's punishment pretty much sucks, how about I add being grounded for two weeks, no Skype or internet unless it's for school. And no friends over for the duration of your grounding?"

"Are you serious? She's like the only person I have to talk to around here."

"Okay, maybe just for studying. But I find it hard to believe Felicia wants to come over when you're pretty much banned from all things fun," Dad joked, his worst attempt at trying to bring down the tone of the room.

"Mike, can I talk to you *alone* for a minute?" My mother stood, placing her hands on her hips.

Dad shot me a betraying look that said what-did-I-do and you-got-me-in-trouble all in one. With three glides, I was out of that kitchen as I sat on the steps and waited for their conversation to pick back up.

"I love how you don't say anything when I'm trying to make a point. I really thought we'd be together on this."

"I'm mediator, Rob. There has to be one neutral voice in everything. We already took away his driving privileges for two weeks, and he's not allowed to have friends over unless it's to study. He shouldn't have gotten into a fight, but let him learn from it."

"This shouldn't even be up for discussion, but Paul seems to have the energy for everything else. He *makes* time for his dancing. He *makes* time for his artwork. He even makes time to get into fights. Yet he's barely pulling a C average in most his classes." The chair scraped against the floor, and I wasn't sure if Dad got up or pushed it back.

"He's averaging C's? Come on, that's like a Paul A. You're so hard on him when it comes to this kind of thing. I don't get why you're not just grateful he's not failing."

Mom laughed, but without a view, I had no idea in what context it'd been. "Mike, I'm going to pretend you didn't just say that. Because clearly you seem to forget how hard it was to keep him out of special education back when he was in grade school."

"I remember; I just didn't see what was the big deal about him learning at a different pace."

Mom paused between her next words, and it brought back painful memories of the past. I don't think I would've ever been more insecure about my dyslexia than when I was in grade school. Whenever I was forced to read or copy down what I'd seen on a chalkboard, my ability to read it like other kids became more evident. Two teachers suggested sitting closer to the board, glasses, reading out loud, but it wasn't until Special Ed was on the table that my parents started paying attention.

My mother hadn't known how she'd missed the signs. Issues with following sequences and telling left from right. My crappy handwriting, and let's not forget all the headaches reading always gave me whenever I tried something that for Micah, at the same age, had been easy.

My mom had a long and complicated history with dyslexia. Both she and her brother struggled with it growing up, and I just happened to be the one child who inherited it.

"Mike, I've been doing my job a lot longer than you've had to deal with this. You don't know how hard it is when you hide behind your dyslexia because you're afraid of failing. When I was a kid, people thought my brother and I were stupid—unteachable. You don't know how good it feels to prove assholes wrong. So, I know Paul can do it; he just has to be willing to try."

Dad listened on, but I could tell he wasn't convinced with her argument. He and Mom had been raised extremely different in that regard. "Robin, we're just going to have to accept we have different opinions on this. You had hippies for parents. I still have offset stress over my father claiming if I wasn't the best at something, it wasn't worth mentioning to him. I feel as though I'm still trying to measure up to him. That tough love rarely works. So, while I hear you, I'm not going to be ashamed of the fact I'm proud of everything Paul does. Because I know he tries."

Something told me after my punishment was over, Mom would expect more from me than I felt I could give. I knew both my parents were proud of me, but it'd take a lot more for my Mom to admit it.

I sat up at the soft tap of knocks at my bedroom door, preparing myself for another long lecture on why I shouldn't have started that fight. I'd heard it enough times today to last a lifetime but as the door creaked open, I swallowed down an ounce of relief. It was only Felicia.

I slid over to the edge of my bed and watched her lay down a stack of assignments from classes I'd missed from being held up in the principal's office all day. I suppose it was convenient that we shared a few of the same classes, but coursework had to have been the last thing on my mind knowing my mom would probably be in here to check up on us to make sure I wasn't engaging in anything that would otherwise be seen as entertaining.

"Felicia, why didn't you tell me that some of the girls on your soccer team give you a hard time?" She lifted her shoulders in a half-shrug as she got comfortable in the spot next to me.

"I don't know. I was embarrassed I guess. It used to be way worse until I stood up to some of them and a few of them backed off. I think he only took it that far because you stepped in. Any other day, unless we're at a game, I don't exist to those people."

I knew that bullying was a part of life and that some people were plain mean-spirited, but I'd lost my mind trying to figure out why anyone would choose to treat people that way. And of all people, Felicia.

She'd let me down gently all those weeks ago on her birthday, but somehow my feelings for her still lingered like a reel dangling over me that I somehow couldn't catch. I couldn't count the reasons how much her being in my life meant to me. How much she meant to me. For that, I was protective of her even if it meant doing something out of my character. I didn't like seeing her hurt.

"Are you in a lot of trouble?" Her mouth curved into a sympathetic smile.

"Well, I didn't get suspended. It could've been worse *but*, it looks like I'll be walking to school and work for a few weeks. And I'm grounded, so I can't use my computer or Skype my friends for a while. I can't even have you over unless it's to study, and I mean, you know how well that one usually works out," I ended in a laugh. From the look on her face, she had genuinely felt sorry. There weren't any words to convince her it wasn't her fault, but she did turn around when I told her if she wanted to help, she could do so by doing my homework for me. It turns out she wasn't *that* sorry.

"Just so you know, starting today, you are looking at The Deering Rams Forward for the girls' soccer team. There's no way I was telling coach no after what you did earlier. I still can't believe you picked a fight with Duke Sheridan. He's like 6'1".

"Felicia, c'mon; the guy's name is Duke. Besides, I've dealt with tougher guys than that at my old school. People like that are all talk. Probably never been in a fight his whole life. Bet he felt like an ass getting served by some unknown Asian kid. They don't call me the 8th Wonder for nothing," I winked. I know we're just friends, but it made my day to see her happy. If a cheesy-ass line was what it took to get her finally smiling again, then I'd be invoking my inner dad. Plus, I was glad to know that she was being rewarded for something she loved doing, even if I had absolutely no interest in it. It was nice just being there to show my support, you know, as her friend.

As she reached into her shorts pocket, the corner of my eyes crinkled as a smile tugged at my lips. She pulled out my birthday gift to her and adjusted it over her eyes. She looked so cute. I loved how my mom got the S's on the side to look almost like wings. I hadn't put half the detail in my own mask, which was why mine didn't look as good on me as hers did on her. Or maybe I just thought everything she did was cute.

"Now I have an idea. From now on, I'll have to assume my true identity because it's clear that people can't handle my alter ego, Felicia Abelard. I didn't want it to have to come to this, but these evildoers never take a day off and frankly, I can't afford to either. Looks like it'll be Sidekick Supreme reporting for a while. Y'know, just until things feel safe around these parts again." I tried to hold back a laugh, but a few snickers escaped anyways. Maybe because she was doing it in that dumb voice she occasionally did for the hell of it.

"Plus, I can always be myself around you," she added. "I wish it were like that with everyone." As selfish as it was, I liked that there was part of Felicia that only I had. Was that terrible of me?

"You know…you have it on crooked, Sidekick Supreme. No partner of mine is going to get caught out looking anything less than camera-ready. Here, let me fix it." I reached in to adjust her mask so that it laid more evenly across her face, only to recall how beautiful her eyes were up close and how her mauve-painted lips brought much-deserved attention to her soft, full pout. There was something about her lips. Something that always made them seem so kissable. I wonder if she knew how much I'd thought about kissing her and how many times I asked myself if that look in her eye, the way she looked at me right now, was her way of silently telling me that she wanted me to kiss her.

After all, she did kiss me first all those weeks ago, unknowingly stirring up feelings inside me that should've been easy to ignore but that much harder to want to. To have feelings for your best friend was a difficult situation to find yourself out of, and yet, here I was, my forehead pressed to hers, her cheek in my hand and our lips closing in the space between us to where I could taste the minty coolness of her breath tickling my lips. It was happening again. No surprises, no ambushes, and no confusion on my end. This time, we were crossing the line together, both of us ready and willing. And just then, as my lips brushed hers…

"Paul!" my mom yelled from the end of the hallway. "Tell Felicia you'll see her tomorrow at school."

Felicia stood, dragging her feet to my room's door as she turned back and mouthed, "See you tomorrow" on her way out. It was for the better I tried telling myself as the back of my head collided into my pillow. Even if I liked kissing her—

like being the hugest understatement—would it ever be more than that? Would we ever be more than just friends?

11

TWO TRUTHS, ONE LIE

PAUL

ho knew two weeks of being grounded would fly by so fast. I told myself once I had my car back, the only thing missing from my life was the weekly, sometimes daily, hip-hop classes I took when I wasn't working and had some free time to myself. It'd been months since I'd taken a formal dance class. One, because I couldn't afford it until now, and two, I had no idea which schools would be any good around here. Call me arrogant, but I had a tough time believing anyone in Portland could come close to the talent I saw back home at my last dance studio.

Dancers from Chicago brought so much energy to moves and made even the simplest detail the dopest part of a routine. You could even tell by the way someone walked if they even had the finesse to call themselves a dancer. Homesick didn't cover how much I missed dancing with my friends.

With the money I saved up from my part-time gig, my life was beginning to align with some sort of normalcy. I had friends, or rather, a friend. Check. I had a job, check, and now I'd be able to channel some of this recent frustration into an hour-long class of advanced hip hop. Level four, the flyer said. We'll have to see about that.

Rivers of sweat poured down my face and back as I reached for my towel to relieve myself of sixty minutes' worth of sodden contamination. I was out of breath and completely disgusting, doused in my own sweat. Not to mention my legs burned like hell, but it had to have been the best I'd felt since school started. Dancing had that effect on me. I'd definitely be back next week.

"You dance like you should be teaching this class." I looked up to see one of the girls assigned to one of the groups I danced in tonight staring back at me. Her wavy hair was pulled back away from her face and her bright eyes took notice, and then it dawned on me. She went to Deering.

"Thanks! You look kind of familiar." She playfully shrugged and bit her lip before talking.

"Deering, right? You're friends with one of the girls on my soccer team. Felicia…"

All of a sudden, I felt a little uncomfortable. She was friends with one of the girls who weren't that nice to Felicia. While she did step in that day, that idiot still got in her face too. Sometimes, being associated with negative people made you just as negative. Here, with none of her friends around, she was actually sort of…sweet.

"I'm sorry about Katie and Becca. Beck's just super stressed about everything under the sun and Katie? She's just Katie. I try to get them to back off, but they're just obsessed with being the best at everything. I just want you to know; I'm not my friends. I actually really like Felicia."

"Then why do you hang out with them?" She shrugged. "I don't know. I guess because they've been my friends forever. It's hard to turn my back on girls that have been there for me my whole life. I know it's stupid. I try to be the voice of reason. Who knows how far they'd take it if someone wasn't holding them accountable?"

Stupid wasn't the first word to pop in my head. Maybe loyal, but not stupid. I hadn't known Felicia as long as my friends back home, but it felt like I had. A small piece of me understood the point she was trying to make.

"Well, I guess I'll see you around," I said, not sure what else to say. I made it halfway to my car but stopped when I heard her call after me.

"Wait." She met me by my car in a fit of huffs and puffs. "One of the other girls on the soccer team is having a party tonight. If you could come, I'd love to see you there. And bring Felicia. I promise it'll be fun."

A party? I hadn't been to a real party in months. I missed being the center of attention with my dance buds. Parties never started until we got there (Okay, so maybe they started, but we were definitely the main event) and I did miss that version of myself I'd left back in Chicago.

I loved spending my free time with my best friend, but I couldn't help feeling closed off. If I was honest, though, I'd have less fun without my partner in crime, so the problem was convincing Felicia to go with me. It couldn't hurt to ask. Especially since Julia had given the okay to invite her.

Julia and I exchanged numbers, and I had this strange feeling she was flirting with me. Make no mistake, she was definitely pretty, but I couldn't help but feel close to the idea that Felicia still felt the same way about me that I'd felt about her. Why did everything have to be so complicated between us?

"Oh my god Paul, unless it's your mom texting you, could you please put your phone away?" Felicia demanded. My phone had gone off nonstop since Julia and I exchanged digits, and while I'd found myself a little annoyed with the randomness of some of her texts, it was nice to remember what it felt like to use my phone for something other than Google maps.

"Sorry, I'll just turn the ringer off." She snatched the phone from me.

"You most certainly will not." A look of realization flashed across her face when she looked at my phone's screen and no doubt, my text history.

"Oh, so you're besties with Julia now?" she asked as she rolled her eyes and handed me back my phone.

"It's not even like that. She just dances at the studio I started going to. She's actually pretty good. Y'know, for a New Englander," I said with a smile, trying to lighten the mood. All she looked was pissed. That was the difference between having a girl best friend versus guy best friends. I actually cared when she was mad at me, but Felicia never admitted to me when she was. She was the queen of passive aggression.

"She invited me to a party tonight," I said, leaving the comment out, open-ended. When she didn't take the bait, I felt it was my duty to press it further.

"Was thinking how cool it would be to go. Don't you think?" But all she did was roll her eyes and toss her head from side to side. Typical Felicia when you suggested something she didn't want to do. So frustrating.

"C'mon Felicia; don't you want to live a little? Have fun with other people?"

"Paul, none of them are people. They're an assigned cult who count on people who haven't wised up to their ways to switch them over to the dark side." And like that, something inside me snapped.

"Gosh, Felicia. I know that there are some people who naturally don't get you, but would it hurt to put yourself out there and let others get to know you. What are you going to do when you're a senior and I'm not around?"

It was a few months from now but the first time either one of us had brought the subject up. This year would be the only year we'd spend together before I went away to college. Fingers crossed that I'd get into the ones I applied to.

"Believe it or not, I do okay on my own."

"I wasn't implying you'd be lost without me; I just...never mind. Forget the party," I said, stuffing my phone into my back pocket. "Let's just finish watching the movie." Felicia got up and flicked off the TV as she dropped the remote in her spot on the couch.

"C'mon. I'm sorry. You didn't have to shut it off." She walked over to the kitchen, disappearing behind the island. When she popped back up, she had two bottles, something light, and the other dark, but judging by the shape of the one in her right, my guess was that it was wine.

I approached the island, taking a seat at one of the bar stools, unable to fight back unbearable curiosity. "Bringing the party to us. Excellent work, Sidekick Supreme. The 8th Wonder is forever in your debt."

"The 8th Wonder is always in my debt," she said as she stuck out her tongue. She wasn't wrong.

"Mind if I play a little music?" I asked.

"Only if you're the only one dancing." I rolled my eyes. "Don't be a sidekick." I pulled out my phone as she poured the clear liquor into two shot glasses. I searched through my phone's music catalog, trying to find an artist we both liked. It was hard. Felicia had crappy musical tastes. It was all boy bands and syrupy pop, but once I hit the D's, I decided that Drake was someone we could both agree on. Soon the music filled the room, the melody to "Hold On" echoing off the old wooden walls. She slid a shot glass in my direction.

"No way are we just taking shots. We have to make a game out of it."

"A game?" she asked. "What kind of game?"

"The only one that matters when you've had a few drinks in you. Two truths and a lie." This was going to be fun.

e were three shots in, as I reigned supreme with having only downed one. Poor Paul had just taken his second. So far, I'd learned that Paul's parents used to play in a band, something I prayed for his sake was a lie and that more than once, he had crushed really hard on a teacher. Gross. I almost had him with my last batch of truths and lies but turns out he didn't buy that I was the avatar of Buffy the Vampire Slayer.

"Okay so, one, I've never had an orgasm. Two, I've tried marijuana twice, and three, I've never cheated on a test." Paul's lips tucked in, his eyebrows watching me with genuine curiosity. This one had stumped him, I knew it. But he wouldn't answer until he was entirely sure.

"Well…you get straight A's, so you don't really need to cheat. I'm counting that out. You're a virgin; that much I know, so never having an orgasm sounds right." He scratched his chin.

"I'm going to go with…" He paused as if still considering his answer. "That you've tried marijuana twice?" But not completely convinced. I poured another shot glass and passed it to him, feeling triumphant in my foreseen victory.

"Wait! What? Which one is the lie?"

I'd caught my black sheep of a brother smoking weed in his junior year, and as payment to keep quiet, he'd let me try it. All it ever did was make me hungry for hours and somehow, cheesy things more humorous, but once wasn't enough. I'd gotten my fill a second time when my folks went out of town and, he'd decided to have a few friends over that were *not* parent- approved. Onto the other lie. I had cheated on a test when I was eight. It was stupid, and I was desperate, but I have since regretted the error of my ways, putting all my precious energy into never needing a reason to cheat again. Darn, those periodic tables.

He took off his fitted cap and laid it down next to him before he got comfortable on the bed. I figured I might as well put the bottle on one of the nightstands before one of us drunkies decided to spill it, and then I'd have to figure out a way to explain to the Phillips why their expensive carpet smelled like a half liter of vodka.

"So, you're not a virgin then?" he asked, tilting his head in my direction. "I don't know if I should be surprised or offended. I tell you everything."

"For your information, Paul, I am a virgin. But it is humanly possible to have an orgasm without another person." His face distorted in disbelief; suddenly, color rushed to his cheeks as it finally dawned on him that I was no stranger to self…indulging.

"Oh…ohh…ohhh…so you…ohh…okay," he said as he cleared his throat. Nothing awkward about his moment at all.

"Besides, sex seems so overrated. What's the point of even having sex if you don't need another person to help you orgasm?" He let out a low laugh. The wine was beginning to work its way through my system, so I had to lay down next to him to keep things from getting embarrassing.

"I can't really speak on sex because, well, I've never done it either. But I've gotten head a few times, and I don't know; I felt pretty good. It wasn't really about the orgasm, I guess. It was more the intimacy of it." He interlocked his finger and cast a cowardly gaze to the room's ceiling.

Paul had it easy. He was one of those virgins by choice. I'd always been curious about sex, but it wasn't something I felt comfortable talking to my parents about. My mom, she had a hard time thinking of me as anything other than her smart girl and has confessed to me hundreds of times that she wasn't comfortable with me dating. My dad agreed with any decision my mom made because growing up with sisters, his parents were harder on the girls.

Even if I wanted to, opening up a dialogue of questions about sex was out of the question. If there were any guys interested in me at school, some of the girls had tarnished my name so bad that no one would admit to ever liking me. For the insecure person (which was most boys), it was social suicide. I, Felicia Bijou Abelard, was not a virgin by choice.

"Do you see yourself being a virgin all through high school?" His eyes flashed with a wave of shock by my question. Perhaps, even a little offended. That was the problem with liquor. Questions you always wondered about didn't seem so taboo under the influence. It wasn't called the truth serum for nothing.

"I mean, my parents make sure I carry condoms and stuff, but I've never really thought about it." Just the question I'd expect from Paul. He wasn't in a race to do anything and definitely didn't feel the need to follow in the footsteps of most blockhead boys whose only goal was to clock notches off their belts. He treated me the way I wanted to be treated, stuck up for me when I needed him, and was the first boy to ever kiss me.

I know it seemed weird because we were friends, but Paul was the first and only guy I'd ever thought about in that way.

Maybe sex wasn't as serious as everyone made it out to be, but I still wanted to experience it, even if it was to get it over with.

"Well, I didn't see myself being a virgin until college. It just seems like it'd be easier to lose it to someone I know, y'know, instead of a stranger." A bout of awkward silence was felt between us.

"I'm guessing by someone you mean me?" At least he caught on.

"Felicia, I think you're too drunk to fully encompass what you're saying." He rubbed his face down with the palm of his hands. Now, it was me who didn't know whether to be surprised or offended. The fact that he thought one shot was enough for me to have a bad case of beer goggle syndrome was in itself insulting.

Vodka was nothing compared to the things that went down at a family get-together with the Abelards. If you want to talk about drunk, you've never seen drunk until you've had the pleasure of seeing someone under the influence of Barbancourt, the only rum my family would ever splurge on.

"Of course, I know what I'm saying. How could you not know what you're saying when you bring up something like that." He leaned up on his shoulders as he wore a hard look on his face. I'd never seen his face stone cold like that before. Not even when he was yelling at Kevin or Micah.

"Felicia, don't take this the wrong way but, you don't get to ask me things like that." I slumped down resting my chin in my hands.

"I don't know, Paul. It's just sex." At least I thought it was.

"Maybe to you it is, but excuse me if I didn't picture my first time being with my best friend just for her to get it over with," he spat. "It's not like I pictured it being this special moment but I at least wanted it to be with someone that cared about me."

"So what, I don't care about you?" I argued. He let out a heavy sigh.

"We're just friends, Felicia. You made that perfectly clear when you kissed me on your birthday. I'm not just someone's experiment. I'm a person." To me, he wasn't just a person; he was my favorite person. Someone I wished I could share with the world without the chance of it altering our friendship. Was it even worth the risk?

"I just want to be close to someone. To you. I guess I figured it wouldn't be a big deal, but if you think I'd be using you, a simple no would suffice." He leaned in as far to my mouth as he could without touching me.

"You have such beautiful lips," he whispered before pressing his lips to mine. "There's never a time when I don't want to kiss you," he added in between breaths. "I know that sounds weird but—"

I took his jaw into my hands and pressed my fingers into his cheeks. "Could you just shut up and kiss me then?" I interrupted. I lowered my hand to his chest and cradled my hand in his.

"Okay."

I wished I could say that kissing Paul was like kissing my brother. That would have made it easier not to want him, or convince myself I was having second thoughts, but everything about the lingering effect my lips seemed to have when his came in contact with mine told me that I wanted to be here, to do this. With him.

I wasn't sure how much time had passed before both of us lay there awkwardly with our clothes off. If neither of us changed our minds in the next few minutes, this was actually going to happen. He went through two condoms before he finally got the hang of it, content with the third try. It made me feel better that I wasn't the only one who didn't entirely know what I was doing, and if I was even doing it right.

As he lay down on top of me, my mind wandered on the *wheres* and the *whats*. What do I do if it hurts? Where do my hands go once it's happening? What if I decide that during, I want to stop?

His lips eased my doubts away when he leaned in for three soft kisses, one reserved for my shoulders, another light gaze on my neck, and the last one paying special attention to my mouth. We gasped in unison at the sign of our bodies merging, me in slight pain, and him? I wasn't sure. My guess was that he was having an easier time than I was.

"I don't want to hurt you. Do you want me to stop?" he asked me more than once. With every second that passed, the easier it got. Eventually, the pain wasn't a factor because there wasn't any. Discomfort maybe, but not pain. I wonder if I'd gotten off easy. The one thing I'll say about this experience it that it was messy.

The heat that gathered in the space between had met us in an exchange of fluids and sweat that told me I would never look at a love scene in a movie the same way again. It wasn't perfect, but the moment was mine and the moment was real, which in turn made it almost perfect.

Paul's breath quickened and his pace increased as he closed his eyes for the first time since we'd started. He reached for my hands, interlocking his fingers with mine, his mouth so close to my ear that I actually shivered when he let out his final hum in one long, drawn out gasp. And like that, it was over.

"I'm going to go to the bathroom," he said as he climbed off me and reached for his pants. I was grateful for the next few minutes I had to myself. I had a lot going through my mind.

The walk home, we held hands but did so in silence. I think words would have made it awkward, and it was nice keeping the moment sweet, simple. I only wished the walk was longer.

"What are you gonna do when you get home?" I asked. She shrugged.

"Sleep, I suppose. Unless I get a distress call. Then I'll probably have to get up and save some lives," she joked. When we got to our street, she let go of my hand. I couldn't help but feel a little rejected, especially given what happened earlier. Sometimes, it seemed like she liked me, other times like she didn't want anything more from me. Now was definitely one of those times.

"Paul, is it possible that if we can just keep things, I don't know, like they were until we figure this thing out. It's just, you've never seen my folks go all strict with me, and I hope you never do."

"So what, you want me to just pretend like this didn't happen? Like we didn't happen?"

"No, I'm not saying that. I just need some time to sort out what this change could possibly lead to. Until then, I want things to be normal between us. Like they were. Until I find the right way to deal with it. Is that okay?"

I had no choice but to be okay with it. They were her rules and ultimately, it was her decision. All I could do is wait to see if I was worth the fight. It didn't matter if things were different. Things were always changing. People were always changing. As long as we could be honest in how we felt, I didn't care if our folks supervised every minute we spent together because it'd be better than sneaking around.

I wasn't like Felicia. I didn't keep anything from my parents. It was hard enough not telling them something other than art made me happy.

"Sure." The only thing I could muster up to say. What else was there left to say?

"So, I guess I'll see you tomorrow morning," she said. Of course, we'd see each other. I was her ride.

"Guess I'll see you then." I turned in the direction of my house, less knowledgeable about girls than I was an hour ago.

Why did the girl next door have to be her? All dark eyes and pretty and perfect in every way. Something about the way she looked at me with her soft black eyes made me want to rush off to my room and start sketching. I'd drawn Felicia's face a hundred times, but none that captured the life in her eyes when she looked at me, but I wouldn't stop trying.

"Oh, and Paul?" I turned to find Felicia standing right in back of me.

She leaned into kiss me and blurted a quick goodnight before making a beeline towards her back door. Maybe I'd build up a tolerance to the way she looked at me, but her lips? I'd discovered tonight that they were going to be my kryptonite.

12

SCHOOL SPIRIT... NOT!

PAUL

School spirit week.

I don't think anyone could forget it approached when you were reminded by Adrian Sanou, *every day*, during the video segment prompts of the morning announcements. There'd been a three-week countdown since the beginning of October, and students were encouraged to vote on what types of events we'd want to see in honor of homecoming.

It was a week that opened the doors to homecoming, and while the whole thing seemed silly, it was my last year to show school pride in a place I wasn't sure I loved or hated. To participate or not participate, that was the question.

The first two were what I'd decided were the cheesiest of all five. I wasn't really interested in walking around in my pajamas all day, and twin day was hard to do when you didn't have a willing partner to do it with.

I'd asked Felicia a few times, but with exceptions for costume day, she thought they were all pretty stupid. My dad surprised me with two tickets to Portland's Comic Expo, not more than a week ago, and there I'd been the Mako to her Korra, but when she suggested us going as Aang and Katara to commemorate spirit week, I was all Avatar'd out.

I was already the Buddhist kid. No one ever said it to my face, but this wasn't a huge school, so word got around. It wasn't something I was ashamed of, but people had their minds made up already of what a Buddhist was and looked like.

It was a serious commitment just like any other spiritual path, but more than once, I'd overheard snide comments about it being all about random quotes and rubbing a Buddha's belly. Like I said, it was never to my face.

That only left Class Color Wars day and Dress to Impress, which was the last day of the week. I was a little disappointed that Felicia hadn't worn her class colors. Blue was an easy color to pull off, and a lot of things she owned were already blue. Of course, as soon as the day came, she wears yellow just to be rebellious. I felt like a dweeb for wanting to invoke some kind of school spirit.

It didn't bother me that Felicia was my only friend here so far. A lot of guys I'd had the honor of breaking bread with were already talking about Ivy League colleges, meanwhile, I was happy when I saw a C+ next to my name.

I knew that I wanted to go to college, but I'd only had one major in mind. For that, I focused more on building up my portfolio and taking on different mediums that were out of my comfort zone. I knew I wouldn't get in on grades alone, which was why my pieces had to be amazing. Otherwise, I'd never be able to convince Mom and Dad that I was good enough to actually pursue art.

My mom wanted me to aim high, and to her, aiming high meant studying something practical. If I was being honest, outside of dancing, art was the only real thing I was good at.

I dodged homework assignments from my English class, the course I struggled the most with and always required a little help from my mom. The less time I needed her at home meant more time I had to work on my art pieces. I'd picked up too many projects but hadn't finished a single one all month. I suppose I had too much on my mind.

"You must be thinking really hard." I was so lost in thought, I didn't even notice the girl with the clipboard, standing right in front of me. It was Julia Araújo. As many times as I'd blown her off since she'd given me her number, I was surprised she could still greet me with a smile.

"What was that?"

She laughed. She had such a pretty smile.

"I was asking if you were interested in signing a petition a few of us seniors drew up in regards to Dress to Impress. They're trying to restrict what we wear tomorrow, but it seems like the only real restrictions are aimed at the girls."

I tried reading the document, but with so many letters to look over without being able to take my time with it, I took more pleasure in her explaining it to me. Her face sparkled when she spoke, definitely giving me some much-needed inspiration, especially with the creative funk I was in. No one I'd drawn so far had had eyes that color. I wondered which colors I'd have to mix to get that particular shade of blue.

The coded language in the dress code definitely seemed more aimed toward what the girls wore. Hell, a lot of it was pretty darn sexist. I, for one, was never frazzled when a girl wore leggings or a skirt that was a little shorter than usual to school. I could see how maybe wearing a bikini to school was inappropriate, but as long as you couldn't see someone's underwear, I didn't see why the girls couldn't wear what they wanted without it being a distraction issue.

"Where do I sign?" Again she laughed. A good sign for something because I knew I wasn't *that* funny.

"Planning anything special for tomorrow?" she asked. I signed my name under what looked to be the two hundred and nineteenth signature. Only nine hundred left to go. She was in for a long day.

"Well, it's sort of hard to dress to impress when you always do," I flirted. Was I flirting? I was talking and laughing, and Julia was the definition of pretty, but was I really giving off the impression?

"I'm looking forward to it, though. I've never been a huge fan of green," I said, referring to the army green button-up I forced myself to wear because just my luck, the senior's color was green. Julia shrugged. "I think it looks good on you." *Yeah, definitely flirting.*

"Thanks for signing," she added with a wave as she sauntered her way to the hallway.

I was relieved to hop in Paul's car after the last bell rang. He handed me what was left of his Pad-sha Rotini, which I was eager to finish off in attempts to eat away my troubles.

"Geez, Felicia. I said some, not the rest!" he replied with a full mouth. I made it my duty to cut off the biggest piece possible because I knew he wasn't one to complain after he'd put out the offer. He took off, devouring the rest of the rotini during stop signs and red lights.

I was surprised that Paul hadn't brought up what happened between us yet. Given the way he'd been acting around me, today was the first day things had managed not to get too weird.

The other night at my house, he'd tried to put his arm around me during a movie but caught the hint when I nudged him off of me. If my folks detected even the slightest change in our relationship, I'd never be allowed to be alone with him again, which would've been the hardest on me since he was my only friend.

"Homecoming dance is this Saturday," he said under a huff.

I shrugged. "So, it's not like I'm going. Besides, I'm pretty sure no one would be looking forward to seeing me there." Paul glanced into his rearview mirror and took a left.

"But it's not a party this time. It's a dance. Who cares about who's going to be there? You don't need approval from anyone to exist."

I really didn't want to be having this conversation. Events related to school just weren't my scene. "If all it's going to be are drunk, grinding idiots, I doubt my parents would let me go anyways. Plus, it seems stupid."

Paul shrugged. "I thought it sounded fun."

"Seriously? It'll just be the same dumb people we see at school every day, with the same dumb music we hear on the radio with the same crappy punch they probably serve at every dance." He couldn't actually be considering this cheese fest. Surely, he had better things to do.

He took a deep sigh as he pulled into his house's driveway.

"Yeah, I guess you're probably right," he muttered as he put his car in park.

I wished I could say it was hard to be this breathtaking, but what can I say? I woke up like this. Portland was prep central, so the dancer in me was forced to take it up a notch on a day like Dress to Impress.

We were allowed to wear hats today, so I chose my favorite Bulls snapback, something I hadn't worn in what felt like ages. Slim fit jeans completed the ensemble along with a band tee of my favorite group, De La Soul, and a bomber jacket I'd been waiting months to break out for the right occasion. Not bad for a hipster.

"Hey Paul," Julia came into view, waving her hands over the crowd. She looked nice in her crop top and jeans, or jeggings. From here, they sort of looked like both. Guess that petition worked out.

As she neared me, I noticed the camera in her hand.

"I should ask first, but I was wondering if I get a picture of you." Confused, I crossed my hands in front of my hips.

"Can I ask what for?"

She smiled. "Well, you know how every day they've been holding superlatives for best pj's, best costume, tallying up which class had the most participation for color wars? Well... today you got best dressed."

Honestly, I was surprised more than two people knew my name at this school. I bashfully laughed.

"Okay." I posed to the side to get my sleeves in the photo. Along my arm read the word "dope", and when she showed me the photo, I had to admit, it looked sweet. "That's sick. I'm surprised someone actually voted for me."

Julia hid behind her loose curls and a smile formed at the corner of her mouth. She hid the camera behind her back as the balls of her feet scuffed the floor.

"Well, I did kind of nominate you. It was the judges who voted for you. You won 4-2." I wanted to say screw the other two that didn't vote for me, but I knew I should've been grateful that I'd even won. Not to mention that someone nominated me.

"So, think you're going to homecoming?"

I shrugged with little enthusiasm. "I doubt it. It's whatever I guess." Julia dragged her feet as she closed what was left of the little space between us.

"Does that mean you weren't going? Or that you weren't going with someone?"

Without thinking, I gave the quickest answer that popped into my head.

"No, it just seems corny, that's all." There was an immediate shift in her mood, and now I remembered what it felt like for Felicia tell me the exact same thing just a day ago.

"I guess you'd think I was corny if I asked you then." There'd been signs all over the place that Julia had any interest in me, even without Felicia's teasing. Julia was definitely the kind of girl who could have whomever she wanted, but if I was letting my feelings speak for me, she wasn't who I necessarily wanted. But she was...

Beautiful.

"I mean, it's not that I think it's corny, I just..."

"Don't want to go with me?" she finished sadly. I couldn't leave the conversation like that. Not without coming off as a jerk.

"It's not that I wouldn't want to go with you. It's just...I wouldn't want you to wait on my answer when there are loads of guys praying for the guts to ask you." And really I was the dumbest idiot in the world for turning her down. Especially since it was every guy's dream to take out the guesswork of knowing whether a girl likes you or not.

"Paul, anyone not you would be a second choice," she laughed. I almost felt bad for the next thing I'd planned to say.

"Julia, here's the deal. You're gorgeous and sweet and so, so talented. If I was thinking right, I would've said yes in a heartbeat." Here came the *but*.

"But, I'd be lying if I said that there wasn't someone else I wanted to go with. I just haven't asked her yet. You know, officially?"

Julia offered a forced smile.

"I hope she says no," she joked. "Chances are she won't, but if you decided that you'd still want to go, I'll be waiting patiently to hear what she says." She smiled for real this time, walking away as she looked back once to see if I was still looking.

I was.

I spent all afternoon thinking of *if* and *how* I was going to ask Felicia. She'd already given me her thoughts on going, but I hadn't actually asked. Maybe she was waiting on me to ask her. Would it be a date if I did, or would it be like all the other times we hung out as friends?

Maybe it would've been weird to everyone around us if we started dating, but it was so hard not to tell her how I really felt about her. She knew, and most likely felt the same, but I could tell she was scared. And for a good reason.

My folks were more liberal than most, and even I was afraid to approach them sometimes. I could only imagine what it was like for her.

Her mom? Well her mom was pretty firm on her not dating, and while it was hard to start an awkward conversation with my parents, I always promised to come to them when I needed their advice on sex and girls. My parents were never intentionally judgmental, and always happy to start a dialogue.

Losing my virginity wasn't the big deal everyone always made it out to me, but my folks always told me it should have been to someone I cared about, and without a doubt in the world, she was that person.

But I couldn't tell my folks that. Not yet.

Mom had been grading papers since the second she got home, and while she was always my first choice, I knew Dad would only be preoccupied with World of Warcraft, so I'd have his minimal attention. Homecoming was a few days away and if I wanted advice on what I should do, tonight was my deadline.

"Hey, Dad." I entered the den, leaving the door slightly ajar behind me. Dad was sitting at his desk, still in his suit and tie, which could only mean he'd been in here since he got off of work. He grunted and guffawed and finally threw his head back, flinging the headphones he wore across the desk in one toss.

"Still trying to go full throttle on mythic difficulty, huh?" He pinched his index finger and thumb together as close to his nose as he could manage.

"I was like…this close! I had a good feeling about this time. Not like the rest of the three hundred and ninety-two first tries." At that, I edged toward the door, losing my nerve to talk.

"Okay, I'll just come back then." Dad pushed back in his rolling chair and reached for my arm to stop me.

"I'm free, son. Seems serious," he said and playfully shivered. He gestured for me to close the door.

146

Dad had this rule. If I came to him first about anything, it would stay between us. If I needed money or advice or anything I knew my mom would've lost her mind over, it was always nice to know my dad valued my trust in him.

One had to tread lightly with The Opportunist, though. Sometimes he gave good advice, other times…

If it came down to saving his own hide and protecting me, let's say it didn't take more than a carton of Coconut Bliss to sacrifice me to The Dictator.

"I …" I rubbed my hands across my jeans and decided to sit down. "Say you want to go to a dance with this girl…"

Dad cocked his left eyebrow as he sat back into his adjustable chair.

"This is about a girl," he said, mocking me.

"Dad, will you just let me finish? Okay, so say hypothetically, I liked this girl and I had no clue if she liked me or not. I want to ask her to go to homecoming, but I'm afraid she'll say no."

Dad ran his fingers through his short black hair, taking a deep breath before answering.

"Have you ever *talked* to her?" In an attempt to appear passive, I omitted some details. It wasn't lying if I just left some of it out.

"Yeah, I see her at school." *Not a lie.*

"Are you two friends?"

"More like classmates." *Also not a lie.* Felicia shared two of my classes.

"Okay, so it's not like I'm trying to scrummage through your brain, Paul. I just need a little more information than what you're giving me." Didn't make sense to keep this to myself.

"Okay, I hooked up with her," I murmured, suddenly interested in the carpets Mom had installed in here. "I kind of like her, but she never seems all that into me."

Dad in all his dramatics, shook his head as his eyes seemed to get lost in the back of his skull.

"You know this is Mom's territory." My mom had stressed a preference in talking about anything sexual. She was the textbook definition of what it was to be an intersectional feminist, and she wanted, no *needed,* to know if everything she'd taught me over the years about consent and the power that sex can have over someone my age and how I shouldn't be doing it with just anyone had gotten through to me. It had.

My dad had no patience for condom talks, or if I was emotionally ready to have sex. His only advice to me was don't do it. The only questionable advice I'd gotten from him was the very one I should've listened to.

"I know, Dad. But I came to you first. At least give me advice, you know, man to man."

"So when you say 'hook up?'" he left out in the air for interpretation.

"I mean, we had sex."

Dad sunk into his chair. "Paul, you know I take it so personally when you don't listen to me. Any advice I give you now, you know your mom is going to resent me for, right?"

I shrugged. Right now, I didn't know much of anything.

"Okay, well as long as you don't care, son. Here is my next set of questions. Number one, has anything changed about your friendship or classmateship or whatever you kids are calling it these days?"

"Ugh, Dad," I said pulling at my hair. "We're friends. Just help me please." He had a habit of rambling when he analyzed things. I didn't have time for that.

"What reason do you have other than your own doubt that she doesn't like you?"

I shrugged again.

"I don't know. Things sort of got weird in the typical way things get weird when you go beyond kissing, I guess. But we don't really mention it when we see each other. It's like it never happened."

"Is she the type to get nervous around you?" That was a hard one. As far as I knew, Felicia was completely comfortable around me. But that wasn't always a bad thing, right? She didn't make me nervous, but only because I could be myself when I was with her. I shook my head.

"And I know this sounds sexist, which is why you know your mom prefers to talk to you, but does she ever make different efforts with her appearance when she's around you?"

"I don't know. She's confident. She always looks nice—" But he interrupted me before I could finish.

"It matters not that she looks nice, but rather if you're someone worthy of enhancing her appearance for."

Since she'd turned sixteen, she'd worn lipstick almost every day. Dark pinks mostly, but there were some times when she experimented with reds and vampy purples.

"She wears makeup sometimes. Does that count?"

Dad squinted.

"Has it always been that way? Or is she the type to put it on in front of you?" If I were talking to my mom, she would've pieced together it was Felicia by now, but my dad barely noticed if either one of us did something new to our hair. It was safe to tell the truth.

"Both, I guess."

"At this point, there's nothing I can do for you."

"Wait, why not?"

"Well, isn't it obvious? You've been friend-zoned. I can't help you once it gets to that point. You'd have a better chance of being pulled out of perdition. Next time a girl dolls up in front of you, leave the room, do what you must—"

I was not listening to this. I sat up and started for the door.

"Hey, kid. Where're you going?"

"Dad, I'm all set. I'm just going to go ask Mom."

"Please omit that you came to me first," he called out, but I was already in the hallway.

"Will do," I finished with a sigh. I should've gone to my mom from the very beginning. That ten minutes I wasted? Time I would never get back.

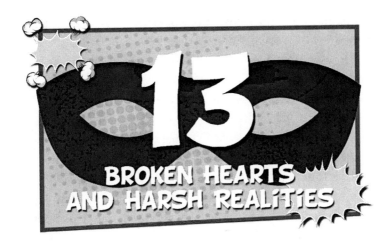

13

BROKEN HEARTS AND HARSH REALITIES

I took a walk to clear my head, but really it was to get away from a certain window in attempts to avoid a certain person. Things just kept on getting weird between us, and I was still in limbo on how I was handling this.

Paul and I had sex. Paul and I had lost our virginities to each other. Paul and I were...

To be honest, I wasn't sure what we were. If I was being honest with myself, for the first day I met him, I'd had feelings for him. I'd always had feelings for him, deep down inside, trapped in some corner of my mind that only I had the key to.

Things were only looking to get more complicated if we opened up the door for something more, and I wasn't ready for things to change more than they had between us. Not while I had more to lose than gain from declaring how it was I felt about him.

It was something I'd never experienced first-hand and even scared me into denying I even liked boys, but my mom was horror-flick scary when it came to my brother and I dating.

When my brother lived at home, he and my mom argued all the time. In her eyes, there wasn't anything he could do right, despite doing everything she expected of him and performing well in school. Things only seemed to worsen when he expressed interest in dating, something my mom wanted us to wait until college to do, if even at all. I remember the one time he introduced us all to the boy he had been dating throughout his senior year. I don't think I'd ever seen my mom so mad.

I wasn't surprised when my mom finally accepted my brother's bisexuality, but because I was a girl, and what she had referred to as her 'only hope', it was crystal clear. I wasn't to date. Remembering all the times she and my brother fought so tirelessly, I had no intention on breaking her unsaid rule. But then, I didn't think I'd meet someone I liked as much as I did Paul.

My mom was so progressive in a lot of ways that counted. All my life, she's looked at me and had no issue convincing me I could be anything I wanted. That being a girl wouldn't stop me from succeeding because I was clever and I was smart. Everything else, though? I might as well have been transported into the 1960s.

When my cousin Victoire starting dating a year and a half ago, all my mother could say was that there was only a matter of time before she started having sex and would get pregnant.

As if no one in this day and age was smart enough to remember to wear protection.

Sometimes, I wished I had one of those moms you saw on TV. The ones you could tell anything to. Or better yet, Paul's mom. Paul's mom totally reminded me of the mothers you seen on shows like Black-ish or The Gilmore Girls: American, goofy, non-judgmental. But I guess there was no use in wishing for something I couldn't have. Just once, I wished I had the sort of parents who gave me a little leeway when it came to boys and dating.

Before I'd realized, I was already at the Phillips cabin house and thought that it might be best to just chill here, do some homework, and maybe even catch a flick by myself. I rarely did that anymore, but the way things were leading, it looked like I might be doing this a lot more often if I wanted things to cool down from our confusing relationship.

Went to ur house, no one's home, Paul texted. When I uncovered my thread of text messages, I noticed he'd actually written twelve more.

Can we talk?

Wyd?

Where r u?

The last one was time-stamped two minutes ago, and while I was afraid to reply back, I did anyways.

Unforgettable Spot, I texted back. The ringer was now on, and I jumped up at the sound of multiple messages Paul had sent all at once.

Ok to swing by?

Driving. If not, take a ride?

Either way b there soon.

He didn't even wait for me to text back *yes*, but there was only so long for us to avoid our issues before one of us was finally ready to address them. I was honestly hoping we'd never have to, but with a friend like Paul, avoiding things was just not possible.

I'm outside, he texted. And with no time to think about it, I went to the door to open it. Paul stood outside the door, hands in his denim pockets, waiting for the okay to come inside. I hesitated but eventually let him walk past me to come inside.

"Studying?" he asked rhetorically at all the coursework I had out, sprawled across the living room floor. Just as I was about to answer, he cut me off with a question I hadn't been expecting. Not after I already said no the first time he'd asked me.

"Look, Felicia. Do you want to go to homecoming with me or not?" I plopped down on the couch, annoyed and too tired to be having the conversation again.

"You're still talking about that stupid thing?" He sat down next to me but didn't join me lying down. He just sat there tensed, like he was already ready to get back up again.

"Felicia, it's not stupid to me. I really want to go."

"Well, it's not like I'm stopping you. You don't need my approval to do something that interests you and not me," I interjected. "I told you before that I didn't want to go. Maybe it's hard for you to understand because people actually like you, but me, I never feel safe at those things. And you already know the reason why."

The more I said the words out loud, the more I realized just how resentful I was of Paul. He was new, he was talented, and everything that made Paul *Paul*, people liked about him.

I had spent my whole life here. I'd known half these people I went to school with half my life, but could I be myself?

No. Could I stick up for myself? Not without encountering the same fate I had now.

I could've had friends. I've had friends before. But I would've had to forget how others treated me. Let bygones be bygones like the principal told me over and over as if that was an acceptable way for a high school freshman to heal while others walked away with no consequences. I would've had to be something I wasn't. Likable wasn't worth being stepped on and taken advantage of. Even if that made me a pariah.

Ashamed as I was to admit this, I had to. I was jealous of my own best friend.

"You're always saying how you don't care what people think about you."

"Of course, I care what people think about me, Paul! I'm in high school," I cut him off. But all he did was shrug.

"Felicia, I'm trying so hard to be patient with you. I miss out on things that I really like to do because when I try to include you, you make me feel like my interests don't matter to you. But I do everything you ask me to do. Because we're friends and because I like you, but every time I try to express my feelings, you push me away. You leave me so confused." He pressed his eyes closed, frustration and anger wearing heavy on his face.

I didn't know what to say to turn this conversation around, so instead, I said nothing, which only seemed to frustrate him more.

"You didn't even want to do class color wars—"he murmured as he ran his fingers through his hair. I sat up and this time, knowing exactly what I wanted to say.

"Wait, is this all about me not wanting to participate in school spirit week or something? Because I've never gotten into that type of thing. I just think it's stupid."

155

"It's more than just that, Felicia. It's that every time I want to do something with you, or anytime I open up to you or tell you how I feel, you deflect it with this anti-everything attitude. I don't think that Homecoming is stupid, and I really wanted to go with you. Unless it's just me. Is it that you don't want to go with me?"

He turned to me with sympathy painting his brown eyes gold. I knew what I wanted to tell him, knew what I should have to keep him close, but I was too afraid to lose him. Things weren't going to fall neatly into place like he thought they would. My life just didn't work like that.

"Wow, Paul; how could you even think that?"

"Well then, fight for me. Be with me. All I'm asking you to do is say that you have feelings for me. Stop being so afraid to tell me or your family. That's all I want from you. We don't even have to go to Homecoming. If you just do this one thing for me, I won't ask anything else of you. Please, Felicia."

I closed my eyes, hoping that if I opened them, this all would be over, and we wouldn't be having this discussion right now. What was I supposed to say? No matter what I did, there was no way this wouldn't end in a tragic outcome for me. Either I'd lose Paul or my parents' trust in me. Losing his patience, he stood up, and it was as if a fuse went off inside him. He blew up in a way I'd never knew he could show towards me.

"Gosh, Felicia; I just wish you would have never kissed me. I wished I would have never had sex with you. At least then, I wouldn't feel so confused right now. You hide behind the excuse of your parents, and I try to be understanding, but I'm tired of you treating me like I have to exist in a world where you decide what happens. Either you're honest and we're open or..."

He edged towards the door, and everything in my body told me I should have stopped him but I froze. I couldn't move. It was like I was destined to stand there and watch him go, even though my heart didn't really want him to.

"Or I don't know if I can be your friend anymore." He stepped outside, but before I could go out to talk some sense into him, he was already pulling out of the driveway. Let him go, I told myself. We'll be no good to each other if we didn't have moments to ourselves to cool off while we rode this one out. I hoped that the walk home was all the time we needed to sort this problem that we had, that we'd been having, out, tonight. Once and for all.

The time read eight thirty when I made it back to my room at home. I peeked outside as I dumped all the contents of my book bag onto my bed. His light was off, and his car wasn't in the driveway; maybe he was still steamed from our conversation earlier and hadn't had a chance to come home yet. Or, his car could have been in the Hiroshima's garage. Either way, I was fighting the temptation I had to call him, but I couldn't help worrying that he was out doing something stupid and/or worse, harmful.

I was feeling so many different things at once that I didn't know how to deal with all these conflicting emotions. Anger, fear, sadness.

Regret.

Regret that I met Paul. Regret that I fell for him. Regret that I ever had sex with him. He wasn't the only one who could feel regret for sleeping with one another. While I wanted to get it over with at the time, I really wish I had thought about what that would mean for the state of our friendship. Because now, it looked like the only way to move on from this moment was to admit the one thing I'd been denying from the second our lips met for the first time all those months ago: I was in love, and I hated myself for being so careless. The only possible outcome was for things to come crashing down.

I'll do what you want me to just…

Just know that things are going to change between us.

I texted to him and then threw my phone by the foot of my bed to keep myself from checking my phone every five seconds. When I didn't immediately hear back from him, I dove to the edge of my mattress, checking to make sure I hadn't accidently turned it off, but while I waited, I sent him another text.

I just don't want to lose you to them.

And I waited. And waited, and waited, and waited. Nothing. And then, out of the corner of my eye, I saw the flaps of paper sticking out of the side of my mattress, the issues of HitBoy and Slash/Girl sticking out between the folds and with that, my heart sank.

We promised to share them, and the only reason he'd ever return them was if he didn't need them anymore. What did that mean now? That he didn't need the comics...or that he didn't need me?

My phone chimed, but I was too afraid to read the incoming text. But then again, what was the worst that he could tell me that he hadn't already said to me earlier?

At homecoming, he finally texted back. My fingers slide over the digital keyboard, typing a reply, hoping that it wasn't already too late.

By yourself?

…....*No.*

Three short cryptic words and I had already answered my own question on what could have been worse.

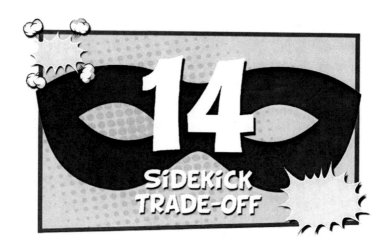

14
SIDEKICK TRADE-OFF

FELICIA

I tried to imagine a car ride with Ma that didn't subject me to being in charge of my phone's GPS or her vast supply of Haitian Konpa melodies floating through the airwaves as words to songs I hadn't even known I'd known the lyrics to left my lips in soft whispers. A trip like that didn't exist. At least with Daddy, I got to get in a few reads.

My mom was one of those drivers who was secretly resentful when the person in the passenger seat was free to answer their phones, eat with more than one hand, and get a good look at the scenery without having to pull over and stop. To make the trip as long for me as it was to her, she made me use *my* phone to navigate.

"Ma, I'm hungry," I whined. We'd passed the Massachusetts state line a while back, and I was sure my mother was going to stop somewhere around Boston.

"If you can wait, I was going to stop by Tante's house. You know she is always cooking." But as tempting as it sounded, my aunt lived in southern Connecticut, almost an hour and a half from the UConn campus. It would be even longer than that since as of now, we'd just made it into Boston. I needed something in my stomach now, or my time as a navigator would reach a bleak end.

Luckily, my mom knew just the spot and in less than ten minutes, I'd be helping myself to some much-needed fuel if these campus trips turned out to be something I wasn't looking for in a school. With three schools to visit, who knew what would be a good fit, but as long as it wasn't in Maine, I was willing to be open.

Hungry didn't begin to describe how much I wanted to dig into this food. We'd stopped somewhere in Somerville, and according to my mom, it was the only Haitian restaurant she'd trust for miles. I didn't care if it was food they heated up in a microwave when the waiter laid down my plate, I dove in, barely taking the time to breathe.

She was right about this place. The griot, a delectable centerpiece made of fried goat and served with rice and plantains, almost tasted the way Daddy made it. Though I'd never admit that to him.

I liked spending time with my mom even though we didn't talk about all the things most mothers talked about with their daughters. In fact, usually, our conversations consisted of her talking and me listening, or better yet, her answering her own questions for me. Because that's just how it was with my mom. When she asked a question totally out of her realm of comfort, I almost choked on my food.

"Sweetheart, why is it that you and Paul no longer spend time together? Over the summer, you were like…those two people that you like spending all that useless money on. What are their names? The something about the boy and the girl?"

"HitBoy and Slash/Girl," I corrected.

"Oh mwen pa konnen," she said as she waved her hands dramatically. "You like so many things. It's hard to keep track of every little detail. I'm old. When I was young, we had only a few interests. It was easier to keep track of life that way."

I prepared myself for a long-winded conversation on what my mom did at my age back in her home country. It never came, which was too bad. I actually liked my mom's exaggerated storytelling about the place she was born.

It was different with Daddy. He was born in Long Island, and despite his parents also being from Haiti, he'd only visited the island for the first time in his life nine years ago. It was me and Jonasen's first time too, and so far, our only trip since the earthquake. But Mom's memories of Port-au Prince were nothing short of magical. Almost better than watching TV.

Almost.

"You were always so close. I like Paul. He is a respectable boy. Always helping out his parents and is a good friend to you. Whatever problems you are having, work it out. I miss his compliments and the little ones always asking me to teach

162

them French." Hilarious since not once had my mom ever offered to teach me French.

Daddy speaks Kreyol. Everyone speaks Kreyol. You do not need French, she'd say. So why did the neighbors get free lessons?

"Ma, Paul has a girlfriend now. He doesn't have time for friends." Paul and Julia. Julia and Paul. Ever since we'd had that fallout, that was all I could fix my mind to think about. I hadn't changed and neither had he. It was our relationship that had, and lately, we hadn't been feeling very friendly to each other.

"Felicia, you always have time for friends. You young people shift around your whole life for boyfriends and girlfriends. That's why I don't like the idea of you dating. Don't be in such a rush to grow up. As you get older, you see that friendships are important. Maybe even more than relationships.

"Friendships teach you about being open and honest. People always tell their best friends everything but relationships, no. When you are young, all relationships do is make you want to be a different person for someone to like you. And that, in my opinion, is not healthy."

There was a slight truth to her words as much as I hated to admit it. I'd seen girls downplay their intelligence to be popular, or boys being douchebags just because they thought that's what attracted partners.

Only with Paul, it was none of that. I was myself. My same old dorky, awkward self and he'd liked me for who I was, not for who I wasn't. Maybe I wasn't the most open about my feelings, but I was always me. That only made losing the only friend I had in that godforsaken school all the more miserable.

It wasn't as easy as 'working it out', and as much as I missed him, I couldn't handle seeing him throw his girlfriend in my face every day. I wanted him to be happy, but it would only make me sad to be his go-to one minute and his spare, the next. I wasn't just somebody's sidekick trade-off.

Despite everything that's happened, Paul had still meant a lot to me, and he deserved to be happy. But I had too much going on for me to let it stop me from going on with my life. Even if he wanted to talk to me, where would I start? He'd made his choice; it was time to make mine.

Today marked a full four months Julia and I had been seeing each other. How did I know? It was the only thing she talked about for days, and even though more than once I'd given my view how it confused me to celebrate an anniversary in monthly increments, it was my plan to make it special in the best possible way.

I'd run down my list of things I was interested in doing, but when she assured me that spending the day watching movies together these few days we had off from school was equally acceptable, I took her up on her offer.

I jumped at any chance I had to save a few bucks, but I thought the least I could do was get her a few of those gift cards to all the clothing stores she always dragged me to. I wasn't great at the names since moving here; I'd bought most of my clothes online, but she was thrilled at the sight of gift cards as they fell to the floor when she opened the greeting card I'd stashed them in. That's what I liked about her; she was such an easy person to shop for.

"Do you want to hang your jacket up?" she asked as we started towards the living room closet. It was warmer in her house than outside, but in my mind, I was still cold and wasn't ready to part with it.

"Nah, I'll hold onto it. If I change my mind, I'll hang it up." She smiled.

"We're going to watch movies in the basement; is that okay?" I nodded, following her to the staircase of her house's lower level. Julia's basement was finished and furnished. It almost looked as nice as her house's living room.

Remnants of Brazil hung on walls in the form of patron saints; it almost reminded me of the altar room we had at home. A coffee table gave home to a collection of handmade craftwork dolls, ranging from light brown to a deep black. I'd never taken an interest in craftwork or sculptures, but I had to admit it was pretty cool.

I'd been here dozens of times and had never had the pleasure of coming down here. I wondered why the rest of the house looked so simplistic. Other people's culture and religion were always something that interested me. Growing up, my folks had told me all the time that it was good to learn how others celebrated faith since we believed there was truth in everything. Julia's family was Catholic, but they didn't practice, so there wasn't much I could learn from her. Still, the basement definitely won the award for room with the most personality.

"Okay, so it's between these three movies: She's All That, Divergent, *and* Whip It. Which one do you want to start with first?"

To be honest, I didn't want to watch any of those. I was in the mood for something action-y.

"You don't have anything cool like Deadpool?" She smiled, putting her hand on her hip. "You and your silly superhero obsession. If you weren't so adorable, I'd say you were a geek," she pouted before crawling into my arms as she used the remote to flip through the previews.

"I'm not a geek. You're just a sidekick," I blurted out before I'd recognized the power of the inside joke. An inside joke I only shared with one person.

"You and your corny jargon. Here I am thinking you were cool," she joked. I laughed but my smile quickly faded when I realized it wasn't with her, but at the times I'd used it to tease Felicia. There were times where I still thought about her. And while Julia was amazing in most ways, she had pretty mainstream hobbies. Cosplay, comic books, and video games didn't interest her much. It was one of the things I missed most about being an 'Unforgettable'. The thing I missed most about Felicia.

It was an hour into the movie, but so far, I couldn't tell you which movie or what was going on. We were too busy going over a few explosive scenes of our own. She nibbled on my lips in a way that sent my heart racing. I couldn't keep up with how far she wanted to go. Without a fair warning, her hands tightened over the crotch of my jeans. Now was the time we needed to slow down.

"Julia, is it okay if I use your bathroom?" She gave me this look like 'nice try', but had no intention of taking me seriously. "No, really. I've got to go to the bathroom. I promise I'll be right back." She pulled me in for one last kiss but thankfully let me get up.

Two steps at a time, I flew up the stairs, making my way to the first-floor bathroom. I wasn't kidding about needing to use the restroom. But I didn't see why I couldn't also get some fresh air.

It was getting a little too hot down there, and between you and me, my history in situations like that so far haven't ended well. Having a minute to myself to consider things was good. Julia and I have had some pretty close calls. Maybe not as much as right now, but this definitely wasn't the first time.

Julia seemed ready to. Like, all the time. I kept condoms in my book bag, but admittedly, it wasn't because I intended to. Mom would probably kill me if I didn't have *anything* on me in a moment it seemed like I was about to have sex.

I guess I was ready to if I wanted to. The question was, *did* I want to?

I knew it frustrated Julia when I made excuses, especially since she knew I wasn't a virgin. To end the conversation, I often found myself mentioning the talks my parents and I prepped for a time like this. Talk about a mood killer. But nothing ever worked like that did, and at best, it bought me more time to consider how and where I wanted this relationship to go.

It seemed like I'd been talking about sex forever with my parents. What it'd be like once I had it. How I'd feel about it once I did. I guess I thought it'd be no big deal or at least less of a deal than it was. Truth was, I'd never come to term with what sex really meant to me. How it affected me, or who I choose to do it with.

Mom had made some good points during our last talk, but it didn't help now that I was back in that situation.

I finished up in the bathroom, using the last second I had to think and wash my hands. I splashed my face with the cool running water to further calm my nerves. If we're meant to have sex, it'll just happen. I can totally do that, right?

I smelled my breath to make sure it didn't stink. I even snuck into the bathroom's mouthwash stash, just to make sure. As I spit the alcohol-laced liquid into the sink, my body jumped at the sound of a loud bang. The vibration was so strong, I could feel it from here. Most likely, a door slamming somewhere in the house.

Two loud, clearly upset voices argued back and forth to one another, screaming as if they expected no one was in the house. It must've been Julia's parents because they were speaking a language I didn't understand. Even though I didn't speak Portuguese, by the soundbite, things weren't going so well.

I picked a fine time to head to the bathroom.

It wasn't my life goal to walk in on two people in the heat of an argument, but in that decision, my only option was to wait it out. I wish I would've at least brought my phone. Time would've flown much faster and been five times more pleasant with a form of communication. Julia probably didn't even know I was still upstairs.

I can't imagine what she must be feeling right now.

It wasn't until the yelling calmed to a purr that I felt confident it was over. There were some footsteps, doors closing, and the sound of someone pacing back in forth in another room. The light from the window proved no more than a half hour passed.

When I was brave enough, I opened the door, careful not to make much of a stir. Tiptoeing back to the basement wasn't as hard as I thought, as I walked down the stairs with no thought to the noise. By the time I made it down the staircase, Julie took one look at me, eyes widened and wet but surprised. It didn't take long for her to break eye contact as she scratched the outsides of her arms and could only manage an emotionless "You're still here?"

Unsure of what to do with my hands, I pat the top of my forehead, hoping I didn't look as disturbed as I felt, and managed a light and weak "Yeah." It wasn't until I observed the room further that it appeared as though she'd gathered all my stuff, not excluding the spot she cleared where not more than thirty-five minutes ago things were getting hot and heavy.

She handed me everything I'd left downstairs and paced to the other side of the room to put distance between us. "I was two seconds from putting your stuff in my car. Assumed you left." If I hadn't seen her moistened eyes before she gave her back to me, her shaky voice would've given her away.

"Guess there goes our anniversary."

I admit, things didn't go exactly as planned. But there was no way, after being pigeonholed into the bathroom, were we about to end our night on such a negative note. "It's still early. Why don't we just go out to catch a movie or something?" I suggested, prepared to make another suggestion if she turned it down.

"I don't know. I'm not really feeling it now—"

"But it's our anniversary…" I pouted. I normally didn't pout, but I knew she'd think it was cute. Judging by the smile on her face and her attempt to keep in a laugh, I was probably right.

"Okay."

I pat down my pockets as if that alone were enough to remind me I was broke. Or rather, that I didn't have money on me. "We just need to head to my house first. I think I left my wallet at home. I thought we were…" I started that sentence, but based on many of the factors of tonight, I thought it best not to remind either of us what might've happened.

I grabbed my bag and took Julia's hand to help guide her up the stairs. I knew she didn't want to talk about what happened. If it were my parents, I wouldn't want to either. But I didn't want her to feel ashamed, or alone, especially over something that wasn't her fault. I kept my fingers crossed that we wouldn't run into either of her parents on the way to my car. Turns out I didn't need to. By the looks of the driveway, at least one of them was gone.

Once we buckled up, Julia was quiet at first. A million things must've run through her mind. I leaned into kiss her as we steadied each other up against each other's lips. For now, that was all I could do to take her mind off of things.

"It must be somewhere," I said out loud. There was no one there, but who didn't talk to themselves when they were looking for something they couldn't find. I was usually good at keeping my room clean. For the most part, it was, aside from the empty sheets of construction paper, textbooks, and all my works in progresses everywhere.

I just needed a few bucks, but I couldn't find anything under the chaos. Julia must've been growing impatient because my phone vibrated in my pocket no less than three times. I thought I'd heard approaching footsteps, but it still surprised me when my mother popped her head into my room.

"Oh good, you're home. Your dad and I received a dinner invitation last minute, so I really need you to watch your brother, sister, and her friend she has over."

I caught her before she could take any step further. "I can't," I said, holding out my arms defensively.

"Stop being dramatic. It's just for tonight. Your father can't miss this. As far as he knows, it's a big deal to get invited to your boss's house, so—"

"Mom, what part of 'I can't' are you not hearing?"

The Dictator was back to her regular tactics but this time, she'd gone too far.

"Paul, honey. I try to be understanding, and I know that you have a life but when I ask you for a favor, it's because I need your help with something. The attitude has to go. Take it down a notch."

Silenced by The Dictator.

"But Mom—" I started. She placed her fingers on my lips.

"The kids can't be home alone. You know that. You don't even have to go see the same movie. Your Dad and I really need you; you're the oldest. We count on you the most." Her emerald eyes screamed desperation, and I knew there was nothing I could say that would change her mind. I had to be the only loser who was bringing his siblings and my sister's friend along on his anniversary date. I hated being the oldest.

Micah was going to learn real soon what that meant when I was gone. If only I could be around to see it.

"C'mon guys," I said loud enough for the kids to hear me. I'm sure it went without saying that their ears were pressed to the door. "Mom, you do realize I have a life outside of this house right?" as the door across the hall opened and out materialized my annoying as hell siblings. Micah's friend was nowhere to be found, but it was beside my concern right now.

"Julia's waiting for me downstairs in my car. I told her I'd take her to the movies."

"Paul, there are about a dozen other movies playing at a theater. It's not going to kill you just to take them—"

"On my anniversary?"

Mom reached into her pocket and pulled out a knot of bills. "Here. I'll give you a few bucks to take them, plus a little extra for gas. It'll probably be the easiest two hours of your life." Wow. Mom must've been desperate. In the entire time I've lived to tell about it, she's never once given me money. I almost fainted when she handed me more than a five-dollar bill. The whole room and hallway was set to be devoured in a warp hole any minute, I could feel it.

"Sixty-five dollars should be enough for tickets and *maybe* popcorn," Mom directed toward Micah and Kevin like she half expected them to ask. "But only if you use the powder and not the butter." Mom handed me the money as I squeezed in between my family to the hallway. Sixty-five bucks wasn't a ton of money in a party of five, but not being obligated to spend my own money meant I could afford to make it up to Julia another day. One where I wasn't forced to babysit.

"You guys, I'm not kidding. If you're not out in five minutes—"

"You're going to wait for them until they are," Mom interrupted. Micah smiled that diabolical grin that earned her moniker well. One day the villain would fall. *Patience...*

An aggravated sigh the size of Jupiter vibrated through my throat as I stomped my frustration to the front door. "My movie starts at 7:50. Ten minutes. That's as long as I'll give you before I come back in here and drag the three of you outside." Kevin stuck out his tongue, hoping to provoke me. Maybe next time.

I closed the door behind me, and only now thought about what I'd have to say to Julia that'd get me in the *least* amount of trouble. So far, nothing else went according to plan, so why should the rest of the night? She'd have to understand. It was only fair after her uncontrollable circumstances.

By the time I got back to my car, Julia seemed more annoyed than her usual self, more anxious than ever to leave. "Did you find it? I've been waiting almost fifteen minutes." I shrugged, trying to appear as if what I'd say next was no big deal.

"Something like that. It's okay if there's a slight change of plans right?"

"Like what?" Julia eyed me with curiosity.

I buckled my seatbelt, with less than a split second to explain myself. I'd only have a few minutes before my bratty sister and brother jumped into the back seat, so better soon than later. "My mom and dad got this thing they have to go to, so they cornered me into babysitting."

I don't think I expected Julia to be happy about the idea, but I definitely didn't expect her to be mad at me like it was actually up to me to say no. "What?" she asked, with a bite that wasn't quite rage or disbelief, but a combination of the two.

"I know. It sucks. But we were going to the movies anyway, right? It's not like we have to see the same movie or anything," I said, quoting my mother verbatim.

173

"No offense Paul, but spending my anniversary with a bunch of eight and ten-year-olds is not my idea of fun." Now that was a low blow. I couldn't help the situation any more than she could with her issues at home.

"We could always do something another day. On the weekend or some other time when my parents are less busy."

Julia shooed me away, crossed her arms across her chest and decided to lean her head against the passenger window. "Whatever."

"It's okay. If you don't want to go anymore." I suggested. It wasn't as if I didn't want to be around her, but not if she were going to make me feel guilty the whole night.

"Paul, I'm irritated right now. If you don't mind, I'm just going to sit here and pretend I'm not here. If that's okay with you," she sighed back. Julia didn't have siblings. She had no clue or any sympathy as to what being the oldest sibling meant, or that situations like this were beyond my control. I didn't mean to ruin her day, but it was ruined the moment her parents came home.

I was confident I could make it up to her, but now she was pissed at me, and I had a feeling tonight would be like sitting next to my mom whenever my dad forgot her birthday.

My phone chimed in my pocket, and by the way Julia was texting, chin in her right hand, I assumed it was her giving me an eyeful. "Can you turn the radio to something else? Something actually listenable?" Micah piped from the back seat. She sat up, sticking her head between the front seats, reaching for the radio before I could protest.

"Can you sit back in your seat, please? You're already going to the movies!" I yelled back. Julia dropped her cell phone in her lap until Micah sat back. Then she went texting away.

"Felicia always lets us pick what we wanted to listen to when she rode shotgun," Micah whined as she crossed her arms across her chest, spoiled as ever.

"Well, it's a good thing Felicia isn't here then," I shot back. Micah stuffed herself back between Nala and Kevin, who were doing what she should've been doing. Sitting back and minding their business.

"I just hate your taste in music. I don't want to listen to rap the whole car ride."

When I got to a red light, I turned to the back seat to face Micah. "You know what I hate? When you ruin my plans. Or when you take your fucking seat belt off when I'm driving. They're there for a reason. The same way I'm sure you were born for a reason. Now stop complaining and put on your damn seat belt."

I instantly felt bad saying that. Well, maybe not *instantly*. But catching the three of them in the rearview mirror, it was all of a sudden an awkward silence the rest of the car ride. Nala looked visibly shaken, and that wasn't good, considering she didn't even like talking around me.

Nala would never talk or speak to me directly. If I heard her speak, it was often in another room to Micah, or Kevin, or even my parents. I must've made her feel uncomfortable, especially with how little I knew about her. It wasn't exactly my life mission to be friends with my bratty siblings' friends, but my parents mentioned it might take her longer to warm up to me since I didn't speak to her very often.

I knew she was a trans girl, but only because I'd done my own research in the past trying to recognize the cues to see if Kevin was. Kevin just didn't conform. He liked fuchsia, and painting his nails, and a ton of other stuff people would assume certain things about him, but he had the privilege to do so. He'd never felt like he was born wrong, just that he liked certain things. Whenever I, Mom, or Dad had asked him about it, he'd just argue that Prince did all the same things, and no one asked him weird questions.

I wasn't doing a very good job at making Nala feel she was in a safe space. It didn't help that Julia kept texting me as the weight of all the pressure from tonight, her anger, and being forced to take everyone out hadn't calmed my mood in any way.

Nala whispered something to Micah from the backseat as Micah countered it by rolling her eyes. The car ride was so awkward; I don't think I'd ever been happier to see a full parking lot in my life. There were parks, but none of them were close.

"Can you drop me off in the front?" Julia asked.

I nodded. "Sure."

I rolled toward the theater entrance and put the car in park. I don't know if she wasn't anticipating, or particularly excited about kissing me at this point, but as I leaned in, she exited the car before I even got a chance. I was about to text her and ask if she were alright, but the mountain full of texts told me more about her mood than asking her would tell me.

She knew it took me a little longer to read texts, so she didn't often send so many at once. But just from the gist of the first message, I knew the night was already ruined.

Julia: *Worst anniversary ever*

"What's her problem?" Micah asked, with a bite Mom would've slapped her for.

"If you must know, it's our anniversary. You could be nice for once; she's going to think you don't like her." Micah shook her head in disapproval, looking especially mean with her heavy-rimmed eyes. *Since when did she start wearing eyeliner?*

"Oh please. It's not even that. She's just not as cool as Felicia. At least Felicia didn't make a big deal when we were stuck with you." she snorted. When they were stuck with me? *Right.* From the way I looked at it, I was the one always stuck with them.

"Yeah and definitely didn't make us feel unwelcome for just going to the movies. It's not our fault Mom and Dad didn't want to leave us alone. I would rather be home," Kevin added.

Like always, my siblings always found a way to make it about them. It was bad enough that Micah's friend Nala was also in attendance, so I knew she felt uncomfortable with the three of us going back and forth, but did Micah really have to bring up Felicia?

"You guys, Julia's having a tough time right now. Her parents are splitting up. Could you imagine how you'd feel if Mom and Dad were having problems?" The two exchanged a look of sympathy. Looks like something got through to them.

"Sorry that her parents are getting a divorce," Kevin said before I corrected him. Separation didn't mean divorce. "Could you just give Julia a break?" I pleaded. Micah tapped the floor with the ball of her feet while The Shapeshifter stood there, nonchalant as if waiting for The Prodigy to bark her orders.

"Fine. We'll suck up and play nice. I just think it's really stupid that you dumped your best friend just because you got a girlfriend. It's not like you can't make time for both." She crossed her arms and hopped out the car. "Nala, you coming?"

Nala unbuckled her seatbelt, and it was just then, I felt the need to say something. "Hey Nala, I'm sorry if it seems like I'm mad at you. I'm just mad about the situation. Or that my siblings were even born—"

"Shut up!" Micah protested, as Nala laughed and left the car, trailing close behind my sister. It was so like my sister to speak on a subject she knew nothing about, but it did leave me questioning. Did everyone else think I'd just dumped Felicia for Julia?

Did they really think I treated my friends that way? Because I was dating someone? That wasn't the story, not the whole one. The truth was I was ready for my relationship with Felicia to change. It wasn't easy telling her how I felt, not after months of denying it. All I wanted was for her to accept me and to be honest with me. So because she was willing to do neither, what was I supposed to do?

Kevin pulled at my shirt, a brief reminder I was still standing there, lost in thought. I put my arm around him, and together we walked to meet the others at the concessions, minus a missing Julia who was probably still in the bathroom.

"It's not that we don't like Julia, Paul. We just miss Felicia. I wish you guys were still friends."

I sighed. "Yeah, me too."

15

A FRESH START

PAUL

We were supposed to be studying…

But studying at Julia's house meant half of the time, we'd be making out. She was so good at pushing those special buttons of mine that made me submit to her presence. She probably reveled in it. What can I say? She was so hard to say no to.

My fingers etched across the soft skin of her muscular back, her shirt riding up as she climbed on my lap. Julia giggled under her breath, reaching her hand to mine, as she brought it to the outside of her bra.

It felt too soon to get to second base already, but her body felt nice. I didn't want things to get too heated, so I moved them to the small of her back again, where I felt most comfortable. Julia always went a different route if I switched it up like that, hoping it'd push me to go further. Kissing and biting my neck was something I didn't even know I liked until we started dating, but the intensity of it all always made things harder to walk away from.

"Okay...maybe we should take a break, Julia. Isn't your mom going to be home soon?" I laughed under a jagged breath, gently trying to push her away.

Julia parents were going through a separation, and she was taking it hard. She expressed her anger in a number of ways, including wanting to go all the way. I just didn't want to take advantage of her, so I always slowed things down before they got too intense. "We still have forty-five minutes," Julia giggled back. "That'd be plenty of time."

She pretended her parents fighting didn't matter to her, but last week, she'd spent an hour crying on my shoulder that her parents were ruining her life. I can't say in the same situation I wouldn't be pissed. The stability of my parents was what held our family together; I knew I'd probably resent them if they ever got divorced. *At first.* But if my parents fought like Julia's did, I'd just be equally miserable. I didn't know what was worse: your parents fighting all the time or your parents getting a divorce. All I knew was they'd deserve to be happy. Eventually, I'd know that their inability to make each other happy doesn't have anything to do with me. Or my siblings.

Julia finally grabbed the outside of my inner thigh, where the smaller version of me rented a condo every day. She dragged her lips against mine and reached for the zipper to my jeans. "Julia, seriously. Stop," I said, taking her shoulders in both hands, so she'd see I was serious.

"I swear, it's like you want to get caught. Just so your parents will have something to argue about that's not each other," I said, in a desperate act of not thinking. Julia climbed off me, buttoning the part of her blouse that came loose in the struggle. I felt horrible for saying that to her, but I was tired of pretending I couldn't tell she was mad all the time.

"You can be such an idiot sometimes, Paul. Most guys would be jumping at the chance to bang their girlfriends."

I held out my arms defensively, despite being lost for words. "Well, excuse me for not wanting to take advantage of the moment while you're too pissed off to think about whether sex is something you even want to do."

Julia and I didn't fight often but ignored the problems we had. I really liked her, but because of that, I ignored the fact we had little in common. We still clicked despite it, but you can't predict getting stressed over school or your parents getting a divorce. She ignored the fact that I was frustrated about getting into college. I tried to ignore her deal with her parents, but like my grades, they affected our relationship too.

"Well, maybe I don't need my boyfriend to be my damn chastity belt!" she yelled out of spite. She knew it'd hurt me but said it anyway. Maybe I deserved it after what I'd said. But we weren't strangers to the topic of sex; whether we were ready to have it or not was something I wasn't entirely sure of.

I wanted to consider what sex would mean for us. It could mean everything. It could mean nothing. But I wasn't just going to because biology told me I was supposed to. Julia seemed ready. She constantly told me she was. But...I wasn't sure I was. Or at least not with Julia.

I felt horrible acknowledging that in my head and even though I liked Julia, I just never wanted to with her. *Was that bad?*

"So, what are you saying," I argued back, as I remembered where I was. Even with everything she was going through, I was still trying to be there for her, but she never made it easy for me. "That you want to break up with me just because I'm not ripping your clothes off?"

Julia jumped off her bed, bolting for her room door. "I don't have time for this Paul. If you're just going to make me feel like crap, just go!" she yelled back. I didn't need to be told twice. I grabbed my stuff, made my way through her house, hopped in my car, and booked.

The car ride from Julia's house left me with a lot to think about. I was full of shame and regret about how I handled the situation. Julia needed someone to talk to. But I don't think there's anything I could've said that would've made fifteen minutes ago end any different.

Was she doing me a favor? I don't know. There were a lot of things I didn't know before the summer ended, but it seemed like I knew even less about myself now. I didn't do anything wrong. So why do I feel weird? I felt like I loved her. Can your feelings be real if you don't want to go all the way?

After homecoming, I'd had a long conversation with my mom. Even though she'd been proud of me for giving the subject thought, she'd been disappointed that I hadn't come to her beforehand. Or that it took so long to ask for advice about it. She talked a lot when she was in the zone, but something she said still burned a hole through my skull.

Sex doesn't always mean you're in love. But it should never feel wrong either.

There was so much I liked about Julia. She was funny, nice, smart. And pretty. My heart went into overdrive every time she smiled. And kissing her definitely felt right.

But sex? I don't know. Maybe I could be in love with her, but I just...didn't think she was someone I wanted to be connected to that way. It sounds so silly admitting you didn't want to have sex with your own girlfriend. Ex-girlfriend, I guess, I should call her now.

Sex itself was confusing. Crossing that bridge before set me down a path of turmoil that was hard to navigate. It was bad enough to feel that way about one person, but I wasn't sure I was prepared to feel that confused about someone else. I know it didn't ring true for everyone, but in relationships, it supposedly brought people closer. But I didn't want to be that guy who had sex because everyone else was. I wanted to *want* to. I just...didn't with Julia.

When I got home and couldn't think straight, I collapsed on my bed, but everything I was dealing with made my head hurt. I wasn't going to feel any better cooped up in my room, and I needed fresh air. I took my keys from my dresser and almost picked up my phone, but at this point, it was weight in my pocket since it was at 5 percent. I put it in the charger and decided to take another drive. Wherever my car would take me.

The only thing that made me feel better was to clear my mind. I had to ask myself what I actually wanted, instead of what I was *supposed* to want. My family meditated most nights at 6:00 p.m., but sometimes when I wanted different answers, ones I didn't want them to know about, I did so alone.

It was so much easier at The Unforgettable Spot. It'd been awhile since I was there. I wasn't sure if my invitation was rescinded, but if the place was empty, it wouldn't matter. It was a place to be alone when my parents and siblings weren't due home any minute.

Meditating didn't always give me an answer I needed when I did, but I felt more connected to myself when I did. I had a lot of questions. Deep questions.

What did I want? What was I missing? Who was I missing?

A turned knob jolted me from my funk. I hadn't prepared what I might say should someone show up to a stranger in their cabin, but a part of me was a bit relieved when I saw it was Felicia. She didn't look as happy to see me as I was to see her.

"What are you doing here?" was all she'd managed to say as she struggled with the strap on her shoulder, laying her book bag on a coat rack near the door. I didn't know what else to say, so I fought for the right words, but nothing came out right.

"I wasn't...I didn't...I'll go," I finally managed as I picked up my hoodie and edged between Felicia and the door.

"You don't have to go," Felicia spoke in a light voice. I turned away from the door.

"I didn't know you were going to be here. I was just looking for a place to think. It's not always the quietest at my house," I said, rubbing the back of my neck. I couldn't make one out completely, but from the lines in Felicia's face, she seemed like she tried to hide a smile. Maybe memories of being over my house flooded back. I didn't dare ask. I didn't want to assume her smile was meant for me.

184

Felicia shuffled from one foot to another, waiting for me to say something before she rested her hands behind her back, gestured toward the living room with her chin and asked, "Were you meditating?"

A low chuckle vibrated from the back of my throat. "Yeah."

"Does that help you?"

I closed some of the distance between us. "Sometimes."

A grim smile flashed toward the corner of her mouth before its light went out. Ever since homecoming, we didn't talk much. It was nice. To actually speak to each other again. I missed us.

I barely had a grasp on English, but since I was a kid, I'd always been good at different chants in Buddhism. Maybe it was because it required diction over translation or perusal. It always made me feel like I did something good in my family. I was always the one allowed to lead the chants, so it was weird trying to teach them to someone else. All words had meaning in chants, so it was why, even as intelligent as Micah was, she wasn't allowed to. If you couldn't pronounce it right, it was best to leave it to someone who could.

It was cute trying to teach Felicia. Even though her diction wasn't strong, I would've never guessed anything like religion interested her in the first place.

"What language is that?" Felicia asked even though I thought she already knew.

I scratched my chin, trying to recall the one in question. "That particular one is Japanese. But there are chants in Mandarin, Sanskrit… we don't take from just one. I can't speak them or anything. I'm just good at reciting. Kevin and Micah don't say things phonetically enough, so it's usually always me that gets to lead them."

Felicia faked a smile at the sound of my siblings' names. Even though she didn't come over much in the past months, they still asked about her. Sometimes, they even came over, but they'd often come back with her mother, stating she was studying. I didn't believe it all the time either, but I didn't have the right to be angry with her. She probably just didn't want to be bothered.

"I know you're not into religion or anything—"

"I never said I wasn't. Not that I think there's anything wrong with not wanting to adhere to a religion. But I never called myself an atheist. My mom did. She wasn't comfortable with the fact I have questions. And she said if I was going to waste God's time, there was no point of me going to church, so…" Felicia slurred the last of her words, playing with the scratched polish on her nails.

"I don't exactly have parents like yours. Where I can come to them with anything. When I have problems, I'm just on my own," she finished, in a sharp bitter tone that made me question who she was really mad at. It seemed aimed at me, I was sure of it. I probably even deserved it. But I just smiled, wiping the tears that rolled down my face as I came to term with my own feelings about our estrangement.

"I'm sorry for abandoning you, Felicia. You really didn't deserve that. I'm just…I'm just going through stuff. I know I haven't been a good friend the past few months, but I'm sorry."

Felicia nodded as if she actually meant it. "Okay."

'Okay' was all I deserved, but I was fine with 'okay'.

"You got into three schools?" Felicia asked, as I fidgeted with the crumbled acceptance letters. I didn't know why I'd attempted to throw them out. I'd wanted to get in so bad, I hadn't thought about what the conversation would be like if I did. Julia didn't even know.

We'd managed to get comfortable in the usual spot, a few feet from the pond. It was stuffy inside, and I needed a little air anyway. "I don't know. My mom wants me to go to a decent school. Northeastern. She's even mentioned UConn once or twice." I'd thought about applying at a liberal arts school. But the resources I'd have at an arts college were unmatched. There were pros and cons to both, but my heart was still set on an arts school.

"I'm sure your mom would just want you to be happy." I couldn't help but laugh. Dad, maybe. Mom? Not so much. It was just five minutes after seven, just a month from Daylight Savings Time, so evening daylight was lit enough to watch Felicia's expression. "I bet Julia will be disappointed, though."

I didn't mention it earlier, but only because I knew it wouldn't change much. I folded the letters into my back pocket and shifted my legs on the grass. "Yeah, well, she broke up with me. I doubt she'll mind."

Felicia blinked like she was surprised then brought her legs into her chest. "That sucks."

From the moment things changed between us, I'd wanted to ask Felicia something but never felt I had the right to after Julia and I started dating. I just wanted to know if I was the only one. "Do you feel like sex changed you?"

Felicia wrapped her cardigan around her knees, despite it being warm for a New England April day. "What do you mean?"

"I don't know. Do you look at things differently? People differently? Do you see yourself as the same person as before?" I didn't need an answer for each question, but when her mouth moved, I listened.

Her eyes widened before she'd admitted, "I don't think so...do you think it changed you?"

A loaded question I'd asked myself again and again, with someone to finally admit to. "Yes. I'm confused all the time. I just...feel off."

"Sometimes, I think you make something out of nothing—"

"Sharing my body with someone wasn't 'nothing' to me," I interrupted. It wasn't my intention to sound so defensive, but Felicia had never been great at valuing how I felt about her. Like I was just supposed to forget or something. Maybe she was trying to hurt me the way I had her, but I figure if we were already getting things out in the open, there wasn't a better time than now.

"Unless it was just nothing for you," I said without thinking,

"Paul, it's so easy for you. Do you really think my parents would let me be alone with you if they knew how I *really* felt about you? Maybe it doesn't matter to you, since everywhere you go, people just like you. But if I lose you, I lose my only friend. I *did* lose my only friend."

"I'm not going to argue with you. But I told you how I felt. That was hard for me. I hated that you were mad at me and that I started dating Julia—"

"I wasn't mad you were dating Julia. I was mad that you left me. My situation was complicated. But even if I'd been in the same situation, I wouldn't have stopped being your friend over a guy!" she yelled in a fit of anger. She sat up, storming back to the cabin. Maybe I pushed too hard, but I'd only had Felicia's attention for so long. There was too much to say without enough time to say it.

I could've just left her to deal with things herself, but I followed her and watched as she fell to the couch to cover her face. "I just don't know who I am without you. You just went on without me, like you didn't even care. How was I supposed to feel? Ecstatic?"

I sat beside her on the couch and buried my face in palms. "I don't know what else I can say? I'm sorry, Felicia. I'm fucking sor—" I hadn't even said all there was to say before a mouth parted mine. There was vanilla aftertaste from her lipstick as it transferred from her mouth to mine. Felicia leaned away before she apologized.

It tasted like I had lipstick on my mouth, so I went to the kitchen, wet a paper towel, and rinsed off the color. I made my way back on the couch and handed Felicia a damp paper towel, as she wiped the color from her lips too. Lipstick only brought attention to them. They never made her lips look prettier than they already were. But I did always stare at them when she wore it, the way I stared at them now.

She must've noticed. It wasn't long before she leaned in to meet her mouth to mine. Again. Only this time, neither of us planned on leaning away.

I rose over Felicia, overwhelmed by the image of her beneath me. I couldn't believe I was here again. The sudden feeling of *wanting* to went just wanting to. There was more to it than how it made me feel, but everything about it seemed so right.

She cupped my face in her hands as her jaw tensed when her lips parted. I tried to concentrate on something more than right now, but by now it was a struggle to keep my eyes open. My mind and body went numb. I don't think I'd ever felt so helpless but in control at the same time. I was less insecure of how unsteady my voice got, as Felicia matched her breaths to mine.

I leaned in to kiss her. My limbs were damp with sweat, so I hoped she didn't mind. I buried my forehead into the mattress, the space between Felicia's neck and ear. My body went into these quick, frantic spasms, and by now, I could barely move. "That was freaking awesome," I said, voice muffled by the mattress.

Felicia laughed, as I kissed her jaw and rolled off of her to dispose of the condom. There was a long bout of silence as we both reached for our clothes. To say to things got awkward was an understatement. We sat on opposite sides of the bed, in the day room like we'd been when this happened before. Before she could get away from me, I crawled closer to her and leaned a peck on her cheek.

"I'm about to leave," I told her, searching her expression for anything readable. "Are you staying here?" Felicia nodded. She'd come here to clear her mind, too. Maybe she wanted to consider some things while I wasn't there to make her mind for her. "Can we talk later?"

"Okay," Felicia said through a smile. She curled her legs up to her chest, as I prepared for the drive home. I kissed her two more times, the last time, she kissed me back. I couldn't stop smiling.

At the risk of sounding like a dork, I had a good feeling about this. I'd made a bunch of mistakes, but I was confident whatever was meant to happen, happened. It wasn't long before I pulled into my driveway. Mom and Dad would probably want to park in the garage or along the curb, but I'd risk having to move my car when the time presented.

My phone was still in its charger where I'd left it. The battery had been too low to justify having it along, and I wouldn't have done much thinking having it with me. I grabbed it off my dresser, charged to 87 percent when I finally turned it on. The hum of the startup menu vibrated in my hand as I waited for the Wi-Fi to connect.

The picture in my phone's background screen took me aback. A picture of Julia and me on our anniversary. I keep wondering what the year would've been like if it'd been Felicia I'd gone with to homecoming, even if it'd just been as my friend. Don't get me wrong, I'd been happy most of the time I'd been dating Julia. But it never meant I stopped caring for Felicia. I just...found someone who made me happy. We *looked* so happy. We were at one point. But it felt like my story with Julia was over and mine with Felicia was just beginning.

"*I'm sorry*," scrolled across my phone screen. It was from Julia. I sucked in a deep breath and prepared to reply. I didn't get the chance to before my phone updated at its normal speed.

Julia: *Why won't you talk to me???*
Julia: *Is your phone off???*
Julia: *I'm sorry for what I said*
Julia: *I won't pressure you if that's what you want…*
Julia: *Are you avoiding me???*
Julia: *I love you, Paul*

All the messages shot out at me at once. I barely made it through the last one before I realized I was royally screwed.

16
SUPERPOWERS CAN'T SAVE US

PAUL

Me: *We need to talk*
Julia: *About???*
Me: *It'd be better in person*

Even in a minute and a half, it'd been the fastest text I'd ever written. I remember what Julia said, but I wanted to confirm I'd heard her correctly. She did break up with me, hadn't she?

I mean, because what else was not needing a boyfriend like me supposed to mean? Maybe she hadn't used the words *I'm dumping you,* but it'd been in the heat of anger, and I knew she was dealing with family problems. How could I have interpreted any other way?

Maybe I was just feeling guilty. I'd been dating Julia half the school year, and I'd never felt comfortable enough to go as far with her. It's not that I never wanted to—but I wasn't going to just because she wanted to. The truth was, I'm not even sure I'd been ready the first time. I wanted the next time I *did* have sex to be because I wanted to and not because I felt pressured to, and I'd gotten my wish.

But I liked Felicia. If she hadn't been so stubborn, I would've been willing to lie to my parents. And even more so, if she wanted, I would've been willing to face the wrath of what might come if we told her parents. Things felt so complicated now. I should've never left my phone at home.

The only thing left to do was tell Julia the truth.

Julia sat in the driver's seat of her car, wearing a shallow, expressionless face. I thought it best to get to the point, making it as clear as day that I thought she'd broken up with me, which I thought was for the best. That wasn't to say we couldn't be friends. I know it'd be hard to. But I wanted to show her how good a friend I could be, even if we weren't dating.

She went from smiling a half grin to an unreadable expression of glass. I couldn't believe how quiet she'd been, letting me talk. I was so sure she'd scream at me, or cry, or do something else I wasn't prepared for, but prepared to deal with should it happen.

There might be lying in my future, so I didn't want to lie now, especially to her. "The truth is, I hooked up with someone. But I *thought* we'd broken up," I said, hoping she'd understand I never intended to hurt her.

Julia's blue eyes were moist, even if she tried hard not to show it. I never wanted to be in this position. I didn't take pride in hurting her feelings. "I do care about you, Julia. I'd been trying to make it work. But we haven't been working for a long time. You need me as a friend more than you need me as your boyfriend."

Even though she wouldn't look at me, she seemed determined to know one thing. "Who was it?" she asked without looking away from her steering wheel. I rubbed my wrinkled forehead, running a flap of my hair away from my face.

"Does it matter?"

Julia turned to acknowledge me, her mouth curled into frown mixed with disgust. "You just told me you hooked up with someone in the five seconds you thought we weren't together, and now you don't think I deserve to know?" She crossed her arms over her chest, throwing her back against the driver's seat. "You're always so hell bent on being freaking honest, the least you could do is tell the truth the one time it fucking matters to me."

I tapped the dashboard in front of me, squinting hard out the passenger side window. "Felicia. She's the one I told you about. The last girl I'd been with before you." Her eyes grew heavy, as she drew her hands to her face to cover the tears falling down.

"I knew it."

I'd done more damage than good. I hurt her more now than when we were together; it was like Felicia with our fallout all over again. "I'm sorry, Julia. I wish things wouldn't have happened the way they did—" I didn't get to finish, as I reached over to touch her shoulder.

With Julia's open palm and the sting of all five of her fingers, she slapped me before I could get the chance to. It wasn't my right to say I didn't deserve it, but I wish she would've expressed her anger with words, like before. I don't know how it escalated from that to what happened next, but before I could argue, Julia leaned in to kiss me.

The taste of her lips was salty from the tears that rolled down her face, and it was too random to predict that it was coming. Julia leaned back up in her seat, turned the ignition to her car on and said, "Get out."

At the risk of saying the wrong thing to make her more upset, I did as she asked and watched her speed off. I trusted Julia, but I hoped she wouldn't do anything too stupid. Just because I didn't want to be with her anymore didn't mean I wanted her to hurt herself. She needed more than what I could give her as a boyfriend, but I was a bit relieved to have done this as smoothly as it'd happened.

I stood on the sidewalk, sorting through my internal confusion when I finally decided to head back toward my house. Why hadn't I noticed her until now? There Felicia stood, just a few feet away, with a look of shock on her face. I prayed she hadn't seen Julia kissing *me,* but it wouldn't matter what she saw, only what it looked like. I think I may have just walked into more trouble than I had hoped for.

"Felicia wait—"

She moved with more speed than I'd ever seen her, from my lawn to hers, disappearing in her house too fast to allow me to explain myself. She was pissed, that much I could tell. She hadn't even closed the door behind her in effort to get away from me. Her parents weren't home as neither of their cars were in the driveway. I heard a door slam in the house, so the only place I'd expect her to be was her room. I made my way there and turned the knob. Locked. I knocked, pleading with her to let me in and explain myself, but the pit of my stomach dropped when the sound of my knocks were drowned by the sound of her crying on the other side.

"Felicia, that wasn't what it looked like, I was—" I stuttered between what to say and what wouldn't make it worse. "I was *trying* to break up with her!"

Felicia opened the door and, in a fit of rage, yelled back at me, "By falling on her face?!" before slamming the door back on me.

"I wasn't kissing her, Felicia. Her parents have been going through a lot of crap, and I couldn't have been breaking up with her at a worse time—"

"I'm sorry the thought of being with *me* is so inconvenient for you!"

"That wasn't what I meant! I just—if you could just talk to me, so I don't have to yell it through the door."

"I'm so stupid," Felicia's muffled voice interrupted me through the door. "I was going to tell my parents about us. I can't believe I trusted you again." As her voice croaked between sobbing, she wouldn't even give me a chance to tell her the real truth. It didn't help that over the past few months, our friendship became estranged. I wasn't even going to entertain that I didn't play some role in that.

"I keep letting you hurt me, and I know I deserve better than that. I'm so blind when it comes to you, but I'm not going to give you the chance to hurt me all over again. Don't even speak to me. When we walk by each other, continue to ignore me. You're really good at that, so you should have no problem."

"So, you're not even going to let me talk?"

"Paul, as far as I'm concerned, we can go on like we never met. Just—go away!"

My world was spinning with no plans to slow down. The tension in my chest made it difficult to breathe and my legs felt cemented to the floor, making it hard to move. It took me forever to walk from the house next door to my room. My aching chest was so heavy, that when I made it to my room, I felt chained to the bed.

How did things go from zero to one eighty in just a few hours? One minute, I was the luckiest person in the world. The one girl who'd managed to make me feel the best I'd ever felt, was the girl who wouldn't talk to me.

For the first time since we moved, I hated it here.

My mind was a wreck. I reached underneath my mattress for a few crumbled college acceptance letters. Something soft-lined and rigid got caught between my fingers. Managing to keep hold of it between my letters, I pulled it out to reveal a teal eye mask.

We'd both had one, mine purple, Felicia's teal, to commemorate our superhero's journey. There was writing etched into the bridge of the nose, but it took me awhile to make it out, especially since it was barely legible as it was.

I want to be with you. I don't think I need this anymore
^ ^

She must've left it in the time I reached out to Julia. I can't help thinking what it would've been like if I would've just broken up with her the moment I got in her car. This disastrous mess, I could've avoided.

Felicia had pulled back her blinds, but her light was still on, that much I could see. But I would be further torturing myself, hoping she'd sense I was watching, and text me or tell me it was okay to try and apologize. The mask and my acceptance letters had once again caught my attention before I considered my next step.

Felicia had made my decision easier. The only other choice was to tell my parents.

I knocked on the den's door and caught Mom's attention. She was grading papers, so I knew she was busy, but the conversation couldn't wait. "Mom?" The sound of my voice made her jump in her chair, but she turned back to multitask while asking what I wanted.

"Yes, Paul?"

"Can I talk to you in the kitchen?" Mom shooed me away, ignoring the question as if it could wait until later.

"I'm sure it can wait until after I'm—" Before she could finish, Dad joined me at the door, forced into a stance more serious than normal.

"Babe. I think we should just," he started with a hint of hesitation in his voice, "Maybe we should talk about it down here. You're going to want to stay sitting down for this."

"What?" Mom asked in a state of confusion. She was still trying to process the information in front of her. Dad just sat there, playing devil's advocate, waiting for Mom to calm down.

"I only got into three so far, but at least they've been good schools—"

Mom pieced through the papers, adamantly making mental notes to see if they'd add up to her facts. "But two out of three of these are dated four weeks ago, and the third one nearly eight. That means you've known about this for almost two months, and this is the first time we're hearing about this."

Dad let out a huff, examining one of the acceptance letters with great care, unsure if he should even speak. Too bad Mom wasn't taking that route.

"Paul, we've talked about this—"

"No, Mom. You talk, and I listen. Whenever I try to tell you what I want, you interpret it as me giving up too easily, and that's not the case at all. I just want to study art. It's all I think about, all I dream about. I don't see the world the way others see it. You look at things and see them for what they are; I see them for what they could be. If I go to a university, it'll only be to make you and Dad happy, but it won't be what I want. I'll be miserable. Even now, I'm miserable."

I hadn't realized I was crying until my dad pulled in for a hug. Maybe with everything that was going on, whether it was my drama with Julia or my screw-up with Felicia, my emotions were getting the better of me. At this point, I felt like I couldn't do anything right. I was frustrated. I needed someone to listen to me, to hear me out, to understand. And the only person I wanted to understand what I was battling with inside wasn't even talking to me.

My mom wiped tears away from her wet eyes and rested her chin on her interlocked fingers. She was trying to keep herself from getting emotional, but she hated seeing any of us crying.

"Honey, you know I only want what's best for you. You're immensely talented and everyone sees that," she paused. "I know you're capable of great things, Paul. I just want you to unlock every ounce of your greatness, not just your artistic side. I don't want you to think that you can't do something."

But the fact of the matter was, I didn't. I knew what I wanted. What I wanted to be. What I wanted to do. I've always known. I didn't want to spend four years wasting any at a state university where no one else was like me. Where no one breathed art like I did. Spending hours away on assignments that would bring me no step closer to working on my passion, and none of the schools my mom begged me to apply to would give me what I wanted.

I couldn't spend another year here. I wanted to go back home. Back to Chicago. Back to my old friends. Back to a place where people didn't hate me.

"Your mother and I are going to talk for a little while, son. Why don't you go and hang out upstairs? We'll come find you when we've reached a decision." He rustled through my hair before I made my way up the basement steps and into the living room. I thought about clearing my head with a visit to our altar room, but all I could think about was heading to my room and putting finalizing touches to all the projects I had started over the time that I'd been here. Right now, it was about the only thing I could do that didn't require me to think.

17

UNLIKELY ALLIANCES

FELICIA

Urgh.

If it was bad enough that my locker door jammed up again, but at the moment, I wasn't in the best of spirits to deal with anything that got on my nerves today. *Scratch that*. The rest of my school year.

There were just eight short weeks until a quarter of the people I grew sick of seeing would be gone. Not that I expected an easy senior year, but it had to be better than this. Sometimes, I wish I had my own personal *Death Note*. But instead of it bringing instant death, it just made people go away.

GO AWAY NOTE

1. BECCA CARSON
2. KATIE DECKER
3. DUKE SHERIDAN
4. PAUL HIRO

I didn't know what I wanted at this point, but I would've dealt with not being confused. I wasn't even mad at anyone anymore. Or at least not more upset than I was with myself. Of all the problems I could've had, why did I have to become a cliché, and let my high school experience be ruined by a boy and mean girls?

I always hoped my biggest issues would be getting into college. Whether my grades would be strong enough. Whether I'd say the right thing to get into the school I wanted. Whether I could convince my parents to let me go to an out of state school. Those were the real things I should be worrying about.

Instead, I was more concerned with whether I ran into Paul in the hallway. The feeling was only made worse by my crappy locker not bending to my will. "Here, let me help you with that," a low voice came out of nowhere and said. Without hesitation, a pale hand reached over and jimmied my locker open with a shake of the door.

It was Adrian. It never surprised me when Adrian approached me; he did with everybody when he had a million and one things going on. "Thanks," I said, reveling in how short it'd taken him to pry it open.

"No problem. I had that locker freshman year. I take pity on the poor soul who inherits it every year," Adrian joked. Outside of the classes I had with him, we only small-talked most the time. I used to see him every Sunday before my mother said I wasted God's time by not taking faith seriously. But I can't say I missed spending Sundays at a place I didn't truly belong to.

"Guess I'm that poor soul."

Adrian smiled, mumbled a small joke under his breath, and stood there the entire time I emptied my backpack into my locker. "Did you need something, Adrian?"

I think what was strange about Adrian was how nice he was. If he wasn't a total church kid, he would have no problem passing the role of the pretty boy jerk. He kind of looked like one, if you were judging solely off appearance. His combination of wavy brown hair, light brown eyes that looked slightly hazel, and chiseled jawline should've made him popular. But behind his back, everyone just referred to him as *church boy*. I mean, he didn't even do Senior Skip Day!

"I was just wondering something, Felicia," he started, placing his arms behind his back. His body language read nervous, but I didn't see why it should. People were never nervous around me.

"Wondering what?"

"I wasn't going to ask anyone, because regardless if I wanted to go or not, I'd have to, being on student council and all."

I didn't know where he was going, but if he didn't spit it out, I'd be late for my next class. "Okay?"

"You haven't been asked to prom yet, have you?" Like he half expected me to say yes.

"Why would someone ask me? I'm not a senior." Deering's prom was just for seniors, but you could go if you were invited by one.

Adrian's posture relaxed. "Oh good. That means I can ask you." Rewind. *What did he just say?*

"What are you talking about?" I asked, trying my best not to reveal how anxious I was this very moment.

"I was going to ask if you wanted to go with me—that's if you wanted to go, I mean!" Adrian stopped himself before saying anything further. But it could have been a trick. Why would Adrian be asking *me* to prom?

"I don't know. I don't think my parents would let me go to something like prom," I suggested. He nodded in acceptance, especially since he knew what kind of people my parents were.

"I understand. I just thought—never mind," Adrian said, before excusing himself altogether.

I didn't use Facebook as much as other kids, but it was good for one thing: connecting to my cousins all over the country. Most my extended family lived in Florida, but there were litters of relatives in Massachusetts and Connecticut respectively. I even had a relative or two in Canada and some second cousins in Haiti who couldn't afford internet.

Most the time, I spoke with my cousin Nadege. Though I had way more in common with Rozalie, her older sister, she was too busy with gaining her Masters at twenty to reply to the occasional "What's up" whenever I saw her name online. Nadege was cool, and I'm not even saying that because she was mature for a thirteen-year-old.

"*Who's the cutie in all the pics???*" I instant-messaged Nadege.

"0_o *Just a friend*," she sneakingly replied.

I smiled. It was probably more than *just a friend*; otherwise, she would've just admitted it. In a Haitian family, it was likely to stay that way. Unless we cracked the Da Vinci Code that'd convinced our parents we could date before we reached the age of thirty-five, crushes seemed easier to have anyway.

Even from far away, they didn't disappoint you. A crush equaled no assembly required. There were no broken promises or hurt feelings outside of the fact you weren't with them. And if you didn't let them in, the mere thought of them made you smile.

I miss the time of crushes.

Now marked the era of being crushed.

Adrian Sanou has requested your friendship.

I wasn't one to use Facebook to collect imaginary friends, so it surprised me when I saw the name. Ever since he'd asked me to attend his senior prom, I'd been cautious. We weren't friends, but we'd shared a few advanced classes. I was afraid someone was trying to pull a prank on me—get me to get worked up about something, just to prank me in the end.

I clicked his profile and was caught off guard by a few things.

Summer in Catalonia

Nothing suspicious about vacation pictures, but I found a part of me grew weary at whatever I'd find in the comments section of some guy I didn't know very well. Especially with all the trash most guys talked about their seasonal conquests before the school year started back up.

Not much was out the ordinary. I wonder what was the decision behind going to Spain.

I double-clicked my touch keyboard mouse, as a video played for a split second when my finger moved by it. Adrian and an elderly woman were speaking a language that sounded like Spanish but not quite Spanish. What other languages did they speak in Spain again?

While though the photo albums changed, the people in the pictures did not. There were dozens of pictures of Adrian with younger kids, and an older woman that he must've been related to, because they had most of the same features. In some pictures, everyone proudly wore España flag jerseys, like they were cheering on a soccer game or something.

I was naturally drawn to the food. I could never scroll too far once I saw a healthy serving of rice and beans. Videos of him cooking paella with the same elderly woman from before made me both jealous and hungry that it wasn't a staple in my own culture.

207

After a quick Wikipedia search, I realized Catalonia consisted of four provinces in Spain, including Barcelona. It was why what he spoke sounded like Spanish, but I didn't understand it. Most people just hear Spanish and think it's a universal language, but they speak so many dialects over there; opposite regions have different and very separate cultures. It's weird. I'd occasionally spoken to Adrian before he asked me to prom, but I would've never guessed he had Spanish ancestry. It's not like I'd ever been there myself, but from appearances, he seemed like your average run-of-the-mill white guy.

He went to my parents' church, but that was the most of what I knew about him. He was cute, but I wondered why he wanted to go to prom with me. I accepted the friend request and was instantly met with a smiley face emoji. I didn't know if I should write back or ignore him, but I guess it didn't hurt to send something equally as vague.

Three little dots scattered at the bottom of the screen indicating a reply.

Adrian: *I hope that's a yes.* 😕 *I'd even take a slow maybe...*

The only thing I wanted to know was why. Why he wanted to go with me.

Me: *Not sure why you want to go with me. I'm just a junior.*
Adrian: *I need a reason to want to go with you?*

Three dots came then disappeared when he attempted to type his reply. Of course, he was showing his true colors. I probably caught him in his deceit! Lost for words huh? *Keep your invitation, buddy.*

Adrian: *Well...not only are you smart and pretty, but you were nice to my little sister*

A short pause followed, and even I searched my mind trying to remember who his little sister was.

Adrian: *Nala. A friend of Micah's. You walked them to a sleepover once. Anyway...she doesn't like a ton of people. She's insecure about her voice because my mother thinks she's too young to take hormones. She's transitioning, so she has a really hard time.*

Now, I remember. I hadn't been over much at the Hiroshimas', but I remember all the times we'd encountered each other, including that time I walked them home. I didn't even know she was trans. To me, she was just a little girl.

Adrian: *It makes her sad when ppl misgender her*

Me: *I'm sorry*
Adrian: *It's cool. It's ok if you don't want to go to prom with me. But just know I'm not just asking you because you were nice to me sister. I do really think you're pretty and smart. I don't think I'd enjoy my night with anyone else, so I prayed a little, hoping it might help...did it?*

I laughed out loud, even though I felt silly for doing so. Before I could send a reply, my door opened, forcing me to close my laptop to dispose of the evidence. It was only Daddy, but I'd be mortified just the same.

"Licia, can you do me a favor and bring up my Turbo Tax?"

I loved how to my dad, it was never his email address or his Turbo Tax account. It was just *email*. Or *Turbo Tax*. I rolled onto my side, holding my arms out in confusion.

"It's like, May. Didn't you already file your taxes?" I asked defensively. But I knew it was because he forgot his passwords a lot. The computer saving his passwords did not help him when he was forced to choose new passwords when they expired.

"My office wanted a copy of my 2014 return. I was sure I wrote off a business trip, but that was years ago, so I wanted to cover my bases." I jumped off my bed, heading straight toward my room door.

"Okay, I can show you in the living room—"

Daddy shrugged, pointing to my laptop on the bed. "Your mother's using it; why can't you just show me on here?" I tried to make up an excuse that wouldn't make me look like I'd been doing something suspicious, but the more time I wasted, the more suspicious I looked.

"Well, I was Facebooking Naddie."

"So? That's not a crime," Daddy laughed off.

"It was kind of a personal conversation." My last attempt at covering my tracks.

"Felicia, I'm not here for your search history. I just want you to show me how to get on my Turbo Tax and pull up a few years ago." It didn't look like he'd take no for an answer, but I still mentally braced myself for the two-three second delay time it'd take me to exit my original screen. Daddy gestured toward the computer, as I put it on the desk in the corner of my room to buy me a few more seconds.

I opened the laptop and was allowed a few more seconds having to type in my user passcode and held my breath as it blinked back to the main screen. My unanswered message to Adrian was on full display. Daddy shot me a sarcastic side eye that was a cross between "Who dat?" and "You are so caught!" as I exited from the screen, but the damage was done.

"Why is Adrian in your DMs?" Daddy asked with an annoying hint of sarcasm.

"He was just asking me about some stuff with school. That's all." I hoped to drop the subject.

"So why'd it look like he was asking you to prom?" My dad interjected, making me more defensive than I'd meant to be.

"Dad!" How the heck had he read the screen so fast? Daddy could barely read house numbers when he slowed down his car to find a proper address.

"What? He's a good kid. If he wants to be your friend, he passes the Abelard test."

I picked up the website he wanted, with the desire to ignore the entire conversation altogether. But somehow, under my breath, I'd managed to mumble, "I've heard no such thing of an Abelard test," and Daddy felt he *had* to keep the conversation alive.

"That's because it hasn't been passed down yet. You're not ready for that type of responsibility. There's too much power involved. You're juggling too much as it is." Daddy didn't try for a serious tone, which both garnered a genuine crack-up session from the both of us. As much as I hated it, my father could make me laugh even when I was going for serious.

"Your mother is always going over there making them dinner. His family seems like good people. You know, when they aren't using Ma for her entrees. I've told her plenty of times, stop sharing my Granny's recipes. Those things have been in my family for generations!" he joked. "You should have him come by. I'd love to see him outside of church."

"Why? It's not like I can date him, let alone go to prom with him. So why even bother," I said to no one in particular. My only experience with my parents being okay with having a friend of the opposite sex was Paul, but it stemmed from us being neighbors.

"Who said anything about date? All you said was prom," my father condescendingly joked. "Getting invited to a senior's prom when you're a junior is a big deal." Daddy shuffled on my bed, adjusting his butt grooves against my pillows. "I half-expected you might already ask, especially since Paul is probably going. But I don't see him as much as I used to."

"Well, Dad, people get girlfriends and forget all about you." To be honest, I didn't even care anymore about what happened between Paul and me. I was bound to make a snowball full of decisions that made me feel dumb before college, and that wasn't any different. I guess I learned from it. Whatever the heck that was worth.

"Licia, I know this is hard to believe, but back in the day, your father was as slick as he was smooth." He enunciated the *slick as he was smooth* part in a way that suggested he couldn't have been furthest from the sort. I clicked on a few tabs, hoping he wasn't about to bring up some back-in-the-day story with little relevance to right now.

"Not really seeing where you're going with this, Daddy." My father kicked his feet up on my bed, making himself too comfortable. He took a pillow from his butt and fluffed it under his head like it wasn't thick enough the way it was before. He pointed to himself defensively the moment I swirled around on my desk chair like he was defending his right to speak.

"Am I telling this or you?"

"I guess go ahead," I sighed, expecting the worst.

"In high school, I was invited to someone's senior prom my junior year. This fly Angolan girl and when I mean fly, I mean *fly*. She had the Brandy box braids before Brandy had them. And dressed as cool as Downtown Julie Brown. She was feeling me too because I was the only brotha brave enough to talk to her, even though she was taller than most the guys." I guess that'd explain why Daddy always had a thing for tall women.

"Anyway, I wanted to go. But my parents? They didn't like the thought of me possibly being exposed to drinking and alcohol, or to be honest, anything that wasn't school." My father pushed the air away from him like he was rejecting what he'd said all together.

"I never wanted to be the type of parent who was strict, but there's so much out there you worry about once you become one. Jonasen, I'm not going to lie. He was a handful. Because of that, we gave less leeway to you." Tell me about it. Jonasen had, and continued, to ruin the program even after his absence. One day, I was going to settle the score. Today? I was nothing but patient.

"But you were so different over the summer. I know it's probably because Paul got a girlfriend, but you just seemed less mopey. I know it'd take *a lot* of convincing from your mother. But Adrian seems like a nice kid. And you should be making other friends. Not just rely on one. Don't miss out on things just because your circle of friends changes."

Daddy was all over the place but hadn't confirmed what I needed to know. "So what does all this mean?" I asked, in a slump, hunched over my legs.

"It means I'll get your mom to think about it."

"Really?" I gushed.

"I *said* think about it. And even if it's a yes, it might come at the cost of a ten o'clock, ten-thirty curfew," he said, talking with his hands in a half-and-half manner. "You figure out my Turbo Tax, and I'll talk to her today."

I tried as best as humanly realistic to stay out of Felicia's way. We shared a class this semester, but I honored her request of not speaking to her, even when it killed me to watch other guys talk to her.

Or guy.

Guess she started hanging out that Adrian Sanou kid. He was cool. Good guy for her, if any. But I was still pretty beat up about the whole thing, and just because I agreed not to talk to her didn't mean I didn't notice her in the hallway. I liked seeing her happy. She was always laughing or smiling when he was around. Just because I was jealous didn't mean I wasn't happy for her.

"Surprised you're not all over her," a voice from the side of me came out of nowhere. I hadn't heard Julia sneak up on me. Her eyes were heavy, though. It didn't seem fair to get into it when she was probably going through the ringer at home.

"Yeah," I said under a huff. "It wasn't...it just wasn't meant to be I guess." I didn't have the right to complain, especially not to Julia. But it'd been the first time she'd spoken to me since everything happened. I didn't think she'd ever want to. I knew I'd hurt her, and I felt it double time for the way I'd ended things.

"That sucks," Julia said, curling her lips to one side. We walked in silence, side by side, as I was on my way to the library but had no clue where she was headed to. We hadn't talked in weeks, but I knew her schedule enough to know this period, she had Calculus. It wasn't until we reached the library's metal detector that we spoke next.

"I hope you're doing okay. I know I have no right to ask—"

"No, it's okay...my Mom. She's officially moving out."

"I'm so sorry, Julia." I meant it too. I wouldn't wish that on anyone, especially not her.

"It's whatever, I guess."

"I was serious about staying friends. I know no one wants to hear that after a breakup but—"

"I'd like that," she interrupted, and I was glad. Right now, I really needed a friend.

Julia had never been good about opening up when it came to her parents' separation when we were dating. I attributed it to the pressure to appear perfect all the time. But now that we weren't together, she had so little issue discussing it, that I was surprised she'd noticed problems with her parents long before we started dating.

Apparently, her parents' issues had been going on for years. Julia just chose to ignore them than acknowledge them. Maybe she didn't understand the weight of what was happening until now. When she chose to talk about it, I only listened. It didn't make sense to contribute when I didn't know how it felt to be in her shoes, even if I did understand the pain she felt in a different way.

The thought of feeling torn in different directions, in the middle with little to no power to put things back together, was heart-wrenching, so I can only imagine the reality of it was worse.

I think the only good thing out of it (and when I mean good, I mean mainly between us) was that Julia finally felt close enough to talk to me about it. I wish we could've been that close when we were together, but I enjoyed being a better friend to her than I could've ever been as a boyfriend.

My track record with being a good friend? It could definitely use work.

"Are you renting a tuxedo for prom?" Julia asked, scooping out the last bit of yogurt from her cup. There were about ten minutes for the bell to ring for last period, and since she didn't have any past seventh period, there was no rush of urgency for her.

I thought about prom. At least what it might've been like back home in Chicago. It was always a competition between my friends and I to have the flyest threads. I bet they'd go insane on the dance floor, never missing a beat. I wasn't jealous, but perhaps a tad resentful, they'd get to enjoy the last important event of high school before graduation.

My time at Deering was far from miserable, but I wasn't sure it was a hat full of great memories either. I don't think the expectations in Maine would meet Illinois's, so I wasn't sure prom was worth the sixty-five dollar price tag.

"I don't know," I shrugged. "I know it's supposed to be this big deal. But between finals and my college plans? A dance seemed the least of my problems," I said. I hadn't meant to be so depressing, but it really wasn't on my to-do list.

I should've expected *some* pushback. It was Julia after all. Her big blue eyes widened as if trying to make sense of what I'd just said. She knew my own issues with my parents and college. I'd been able to voice them over the past week weeks, and she did the courtesy of listening in my time of need, too. But this wasn't one of those things Julia would ignore.

"It's not just a dance. It's prom."

"I'm sure there'll be other stuff to look forward to," I said in a nonchalant tone, hoping she'd drop it.

"But you only get one prom, Paul. Years from now, you'll be kicking yourself in the butt for not going. I know it's not Chicago, but the least you could do is make the most of the time you actually did spend in Portland." She'd managed all that in one breath. This is why you didn't have friends involved in school-related events. They'll always try to convince you to do *everything*.

"I guess."

"Do you not want to go because you can't go with Felicia?" Of course, she'd open that wound, but we'd gotten past it. I didn't deserve Julia's forgiveness, but I certainly didn't mind her not hating me for the rest of my life.

"I don't know. Maybe. But I just don't want to be around everyone having fun, and I'm just sitting there by myself."

"Why don't I take you?" Julia offered, but within seconds tried to clarify herself. "I mean, not like that. As friends. I'm going anyway, but I know I'd never forgive myself if I knew you weren't going just because you feel like Portland wasn't home to you." Home was where your family was. Portland was as in me as Chicago had been, doubled by the fact it surrounded by my parents and siblings. Wherever I went, whether I liked to admit it or not, this was always going to be a part of me too.

I should have some decent memories of it. Months ago, it would've been no question to go with Julia. But now that we were just friends? I didn't see why we couldn't make a weird situation into a decent one.

"All I want to know is who's renting the limo?"

18

WHOEVER SAID EXES CAN'T BE ALLIES?

PAUL

I f I never saw another flash from a camera again, I swear it would be too soon. My dad liked to imagine that in another universe, he was some sort of Parisian photographer, the go-to for all the famous print shoot models, and it was his goal to blind us whenever my siblings and I got all dressed up for an event.

Don't get me wrong, I was known to indulge in a well-lit selfie or two (or hundred) myself, but it was getting a little on the embarrassing side seeing my dad on the floor trying to capture me and Julia at every angle he could manage without pulling something. The *Yas Dahling* accent wasn't helping either.

"C'mon, Dad. Julia and I have taken enough pictures to last a lifetime. We've got to get going. I'm sure the others will be here any minute."

Julia, who was hell bent on seeing some of the photos my dad snapped, laid down on the floor next to him, pointing out the ones she'd want for her own personal collection. But as much as I'd paid for the suit I was wearing, every minute we'd spent on my living room floor was a minute no one was seeing my stylish trends.

I felt like James Bond, only younger and fresher, and I mean, who was I kidding, sexier too, I thought as I adjusted my dark blue bowtie in our hallway mirror.

"That's why your date is taller than you with heels on," Micah crept up, laughing as though she had somehow convinced herself that her petty words got to me. Wasn't going to work, though; if there were ever a time I was feeling myself way too hard, tonight was that night.

"I'm only kidding. You actually look like a decent human being. Try to get home before midnight, though; you know there's a huge chance of you trying back into a rat," she casually tossed before flipping her hair and heading back into the living room. So, I officially had The Prodigy's stamp of approval. Backhanded or not, that was the best I was ever going to get with my bratty little sister.

I looked at my watch as my eyes bugged out at the time, and then to make matters worse, the doorbell rang. It was probably all of Julia's friends waiting outside to pick us up. Without thinking, I ran to the door to tell them to give us a second as we finalized our looks and said our final goodbyes to my family, but when I opened the door, it wasn't them. It was Adrian Sanou, holding a clear case, home to a white corsage.

Like me, he was wearing a well-tailored suit instead of a tuxedo, but instead of the dark blue accents I wore on mine, his were a light purple. Cool combination. Something I would've done.

"Oh hey, Paul. I think I may have gotten the houses mixed up or something. At least I won't be the only one to forgo the tux."

My chest tightened as a constricting pressure that started at the base of my throat made it suddenly hard to talk. I thought there was a chance he might ask her. Seeing him here made my worst nightmare a heartbreaking reality. I faked a smile.

"Right street, wrong house. Felicia's next door. Try not to get lost on your way there this time," I ended with a laugh. Adrian wasn't a bad guy. I actually kind of liked him. But he was taking Felicia to my senior prom when I wished it were me instead.

We exchanged our goodbyes as I closed the door behind him, nursing a deep breath as I wondered if I was strong enough to go through with this. I was going to have fun, and I was going with someone who promised to make sure I did even if it had been my every intention to mope. Tonight, that was all I could ask for.

Julia came rushing to the door to tell me that her friends were going to be here soon, so we put on our shoes ,and within seconds, they were pulling up out front.

She really was noticeably taller than me with her heels on, but she looked so stunning tonight, in her pale pink layered dress, I knew no one else was going to bring attention to it. Besides, it's not like it was my fault that taller girls dug me.

After seeing everyone off, hand in hand, we glided to the limo. I'd really hoped to see how Felicia had looked. Sure, I had planned to have fun despite of it all, but what I just really wanted was a chance to confront her and make good on all the bad blood brewing between us.

Man, if I ever needed a reason to regret wishing I could rewind time so I'd be back in Chicago, the sight of this reception had definitely been one of them.

With the intent not to show my resentment, I tried not to showcase the envy I'd felt at the sound of my friends discussing their senior prom's details through our last few Skype conversations over the weeks.

It was both hilarious and upsetting that my old school decided on a steampunk-western theme a la Wild, Wild West. It sounded about as cheesy as it did fun, and I couldn't help but imagine what it'd be like if we'd all gotten to experience it together at our last school-related function outside of graduation.

I didn't think prom in Portland would be a total drag, especially since Julia's agreed to go with me, but any other doubts I'd been harboring melted away the moment we arrived at Portland Ocean Gateway, the venue where prom was being held.

It was known for its wedding receptions, but I bet after this event, more and more high schools would be looking to throw any school dance here, especially with its view of the water. That made it the best reflection of Maine. The only thing that could've made it better was if we'd all been allowed to bring bathing suits.

But if that'd been all there was to look forward to, I could've just gasped now. The closer we all got to the ball-room where the ceremony was being held, the more the on-set hyperventilating started to kick in, and any minute, I feared I'd lose my breath.

Deering's movie premiere theme had the possibility of being campy, but just from the hallway alone, it was at the very least, inviting. There was a red carpet-style hallway that lead to the doorway of the ballroom, but the way everything was set up, one couldn't imagine all the effort it took to achieve the look.

Papier-Mache statues of Oscars, SAGs, and Emmys were dressed in each corner, as a huge film roll-style counter table of attendants who went to our school were taking tickets at the entrance. They were dressed in usher-style uniforms, with huge engaging smiles every time someone passed. I had to wonder if they were so happy to be missing prom or just happy to be a part of it in some way, even if crowds weren't their thing.

"Oh, let's flex for the camera!" Julia teased, as the red wall across from the entrance was an unofficial paparazzi-style display where a student taking pictures pretended anyone walking by was a real celebrity. Julia and I did our best to be classy for the first set of pics, but it went all downhill the moment we started making dumb faces and poses as I summoned my best 8th Wonder pose.

Julia mentioned being one of the many members of the prom committee, so while I'd expected something nice, I didn't expect for it to look *this* upscale. "Wow, Julia. Prom committee did a really good job." As I pat her on the back, she giggled at the compliment.

"Trust me; this was way better than anyone expected it to be. The budget gave us so little to do with, so if you want to thank anyone, thank the volunteers from other grades. They really showed up."

I had to remember that. A part of me was looking forward to talking to a junior right now, but I had to spot her first before I could do anything. Until then, I couldn't do anything from out here. The sounds of *Rich Homie Quan* swelled and diminished every time the entrance of prom opened and closed, and if I didn't hurry, all my favorite songs would end before I got to dance to them.

I took Julia's wrist and dragged her over to the ticket booth before we could miss another minute of the party going on inside. "Party of two?" the attendant asked before placing two swag bags on their counter, inviting us to take one apiece and head on inside.

"What are these?" I asked as we walked and talked.

Julia pulled out a neatly rolled up Deering High t-shirt, along with other school or prom- related trinkets they'd managed to squeeze inside. "You must not follow *any* award shows. The committee thought swag bags would be a cute touch to the hundred-thousand-dollar swag bags celebrities get for attending the Grammys or the Oscars."

Julia continued to reach inside, pulling out anything from mini-popcorn holders to tiny Hollywood director's tape toys, as the rest were pens, pencils, or small stationary with the Deering logo on it. I thought it best not to open mine, considering Julia had so much trouble trying to get everything back in than she did taking it out.

I let the DJ's amplified voice lead us forward onto the crowded dance floor as we squeezed through to look around.

The further I checked it out, the more the movie premiere theme was on point.

Red, black, gold, and white balloons were scattered everywhere, as couples lined up to the picture booth inside, as mementos in the school yearbook. I wanted to grab a shot, but it seemed best to wait for the line to die done a bit, so we could get the rest of the view of the venue before settling down at a table.

Each table followed the theme as prom, with Hollywood director's tape balloons and placement holders as centerpieces. It definitely accentuated the black, red, or gold table clothes and napkins on each plate to contrast each table. Even the chairs were Hollywood-themed. You know those fold-in cast chairs people used when they were on sets? Each chair mirrored that, only there was a glitter glue pen attached to the side of each chair, so people could write their names on the back as if prom was its own set.

Looking at everything now, I was so glad I hadn't stayed home. Outside of my plan to turn up, if I hadn't come then I'd have nothing to brag about to my friends back in Chicago the next time we Skyped, and *that* would truly be a missed opportunity.

The room's temperature rose from the moment I stepped in, through the course of a mere hour. It wasn't for nothing, though; the DJ was on fire. The guy made it hard for me to sit still and rest my feet. I couldn't resist a radio favorite, and with the selection, it looked like I wouldn't sit down the entire night.

I'd never used school dances back in Illinois as a chance to dance with girls—unless they were willing to battle me first. So, I thought it'd feel unnatural to go against the typical bump and grind you normally seen at dances.

Deering had always been in the lacking department when it came to a people who'd actually had rhythm, so for the longest time, I'd buried my love for it, along with everything else I tied back to Chicago. Yet here I was, trying to teach a fellow classmate *The Quan*. I'm glad I planned ahead, opting to pack sneakers along with my dress shoes. It could be done, but anytime you six-stepped in a pair of shoes with little traction, hazards were known to happen.

"Dude, I didn't know you could dance like that!" repeated over and over among half my graduating class, and Julia was definitely reaping some of the benefits. I remember teaching her a few pop and lock moves back when we were dating, and her attempts at a few trap songs proved she wasn't half bad at them.

I was glad we'd been able to put our past behind us and not let it stand in the way of ruining our good time. I still liked her, even if it were just as a friend. If she would've missed this because of me, it probably would've haunted me for all of eternity. *Or at least until I graduated from college.* By then, I'd have to deal with the real world, but right now? I got to savor the last moment of high school that'd really meant something to me.

The night was going so well, I had to dust myself off. In fact, the only way I could've had more fun was if I'd gone with...

And then I saw them.

226

I should've known this moment was coming. My only wish is that I'd prepared myself for it. For the first time all night, I'd finally seen who I'd been looking for, and it was the only time I'd felt less than the usual me.

Felicia.

With Adrian.

I wasn't sure if they'd been here as long as I had, or just arrived; I just hoped I'd have a little longer to come to terms with everything.

She looked pretty. I was glad I got to bear witness to that at least once at some point, but it definitely left my confidence level at a standstill. I couldn't help but sink a little at the sight of her not with me.

Come on, a slow song? Why'd they have to play a song like that right now? *Urgh*, the DJ was officially on my bad list. Why couldn't he just stick to upbeat songs? Okay, that was selfish. I'm sure all the couples were just looking for their turn to own the dance floor. Didn't take away from the fact that it sucked.

Not that the idea of slow dancing with Julia sucked; we had dated, and I was no stranger to being this close to her. It was the fact that I was a few feet short of view of Felicia being asked to dance. Not exactly a mood elevator. It's not like I was jealous—okay, maybe I was a teeny bit jealous. But I was more upset with myself than I could ever be jealous.

Everything that lead up to now might've been different if I hadn't made so many mistakes. It wasn't Felicia's fault I'd messed up. If things would've gone differently, I would've told her how I felt about everything—and not just what happened a few weeks back. I held an undeniable amount of regret when it came to the decline of our friendship. As much as I'd let go since the last time we talked, there was still a small part that missed her, our friendship, and anything we could've been.

"If I'd known you were going to burn a hole through the both of them, I would've made sure my dress was fireproof," Julia snickered, pulling me out my drunken daze. Damn, I couldn't do anything right. Here I was, supposedly trying to make up for all the crap I'd put not only Felicia through, but Julia too, and all I could seem to do was subject her to watching me watching Felicia dance with Adrian.

"Gosh, Julia. I'm so sorry. I'm totally being a jerk. I'll be in fighting shape in a second. I'm just thrown off my game, that's all."

Julia didn't buy it. She rolled her eyes at me, shooing me away like I'd said something annoying or something. "I was just *joking*, Paul. I didn't realize you'd be so *sensitive* about it," she said, putting stress towards the last of each sentence.

I put on a fake smile, convinced it was all she needed to forget it happened. "Seriously, though. It won't happen again."

Okay, now I *knew* Julia wasn't buying it. With one cock of her brow, her look radiated superiority. There was no way she was that stupid. "Are you kidding me? Yes, it will. But if you plan on eye-boinking her all night, the least you could do is ask her to dance—"

"*What*? No!" I interrupted.

"Wow. All this pushback for *one* dance?"

I gestured my hand in the direction of the dancefloor. "Look at her. She's clearly doing her own thing. Why ruin it?"

Julia crossed her arms and, with such exaggeration, you'd think I'd been pinching her all night. "I swear; guys are such wimps these days. If I hadn't asked you out, I would've still been standing in that hallway. If you like her, standing over here is never going to change anything."

228

Julia was definitely bolder than girls I'd dated before, and while I agreed with her, I was at a loss of what to do. I shrugged in the direction of Adrian and Felicia. "What am I supposed to do? *Cut in?*"

"You're freaking hopeless." Julia lightly slapped her palm against my forehead and laughed. "Just wait for this song to end and watch."

At this point, there was nothing but relief running through my body at the song finally ending. I knew it was asking too much, but a long stretch between hyping the crowd and fast paced music would definitely be appreciated.

Julia was planning something, but she was tight-lipped when I'd asked about it. It didn't matter anyway because I wouldn't have been paying attention. Adrian reached over and yelled something over the music into Felicia's ear. Whatever he'd said, she'd mutually agreed on, because they squeezed through the crowd in opposite directions, Felicia toward the ballroom exit and Adrian toward the refreshment table. Julia took one more glance over her shoulder, and in a full-lipped grin teased, "This is why you *need* me," as she took no time gliding toward Adrian's direction.

I wasn't sure if Julia wanted me to wait for a signal or something, but before I could come up with an idea of what she was planning, she reached in for a cup, poured herself a drink, and, spilled the contents of the cup all over Adrian's jacket. "Oops," was all I heard before I rushed over to offer my help, not expecting Adrian's jacket might become the innocent bystander in the effort to speak to Felicia.

"Oh my god, Adrian, I'm so sorry!" As Julia's lips stretched into a grimace, I grabbed a few napkins off the table and offered them to Adrian, but I wasn't sure how much good they'd do at this point.

"You okay, man?"

Adrian reached out for the offered napkins, lightly dabbing them against his jacket's fabric. "I guess."

"Again, I'm *so* sorry Adrian. I didn't see you there," Julia pleaded, playing it off as well as any Hollywood actress.

"It's okay, it's just…my mom's probably going to kill me."

"I have stain removal wipes in my purse, but it's downstairs at the check-in counter. Come with me, and I'll help you get it out. I feel horrible Adrian; I don't want you to get in trouble or anything."

Adrian peeled his jacket away from him, and I couldn't have felt worse about putting him in this situation.

"I guess I have to. Hey, Paul? Could you do me a favor?"

"Anything," I assured, trying to not show the weight of guilt my pockets were carrying.

"Felicia wanted some fresh air, and I told her I'd bring a drink out to her. Could you tell her I'll be right back? I don't want her to think I just left her there to wait by herself."

"Sure, man."

Julia scowled in my direction, as she pulled Adrian by the wrist out of the ballroom. I had to remind myself to both thank and let her have it for earning me a moment of Felicia's time. I figured I'd only have a few minutes before Adrian came to look for her, and even if an encounter didn't bring the outcome I wanted, I had my shot. So I was taking it.

The therapeutic effect I'd gotten from inhaling the fresh sea air only heightened when I got a good look around from the outside balcony. This had to be one of the most beautiful waterfronts I'd yet to set eyes on. It was nothing short of amazing with its all-encompassing view of the Atlantic and the occasional sailboat drifting by on the dark, glittering surface. Although she wasn't the only one out here, Felicia was easy to spot. She was the only girl wearing purple, not to mention the only girl wearing her hair in a crown full of curls and kinks that made up her hair's natural texture. She was in her own league of self-confidence, her hair being only a small fraction of the carefree beauty she possessed.

As I approached the rail of the balcony she leaned on, I'd noticed her heels in her hands, which made me laugh to myself. With all the dancing girls had to do in those things, it was a wonder why they even wore them to prom. Why not skip them altogether?

"Hey," I said as she briefly turned towards me. The look on her face said it all like she was expecting someone else, and I quickly had to remind myself that she did come here with someone else. Why would she be expecting to see me?

"Hi," she finally answered back. Unsure of what more to say, I stood there, directing my eyes towards the body of water in front of me. As we gazed out into the sea in silence, I remembered that I would only have a small window of time to talk to her before Adrian came looking for her. I didn't want to make a scene here; I owed Adrian that much. To me, he had always been an okay guy.

"You look really pretty, Felicia."

"Thanks. You look really nice, too," she said, although barely looking at me. Was it naïve to think we could just go back in time to a point where I accepted how she felt all those months back and accepted what we had on her terms? I didn't want to leave tonight believing she hated me, even though I'd given her a million and one reasons to do so. If there was still a chance we could be friends, I'd never know if I didn't say something. There were only a few weeks left in the semester, and a few months away was a long time for my mind to think about never having a final conversation about where our relationship stood.

"I wish it were me you came with tonight. I know we would have had a blast together." She shrugged.

"I don't know. Maybe," she said with less enthusiasm than I'd hoped. Maybe this was the end for us. Perhaps she wasn't the same Felicia. The one before I had hurt her. This version, all new and out of her element, didn't want to be bothered with my attempts to lighten the mood. This one didn't have many words for me. This Felicia…

This Felicia was over me.

I gathered what pride I had left, deciding that it was time to find my date. For the first time all night, I wasn't having much fun. I couldn't wait for this night to be over.

"You know, seeing you tonight made me understand something," she started before I'd taken the full plunge of walking away. There was a chance that whatever she'd planned on saying to me was going to make me feel worse than I did, but I was a glutton for punishment.

"This scene. This environment. This is *you*. You're so comfortable being the person that everyone likes. The one that everyone finds funny. The one no one can outdo when it comes to being cool, and I'm…" she paused. "Well, I'm just me."

"You say that like it's a bad thing," I argued.

"I don't mean it in a bad way. It's just…all night, it just had me thinking about how the friend you were to me, I'm not sure if I was being the same friend to you. I could've been better."

This time, she finally looked at me, and it was then I knew that the decision I'd made to go away next fall for school, I would never get over it. Even if she was the reason why I left, she was also reason enough for me to stay. And here she was, apologizing to me as if she were the one who'd hurt me more than I'd hurt her. I didn't deserve her as my friend.

"I never wanted to keep you from the world. I know as people, we don't really belong to one another, but I just wanted you all to myself. I liked you because you *are* that person. Someone who sees the best in people. Someone who saw the best in me," she trailed off. "I guess what I'm trying to say is, I'm sorry. For everything. Maybe if I had been a braver person, things could have been different," she finally said before she made an attempt to walk away. Maybe we could never be what we were, but that wasn't a bad thing. There was always the hope in something new. Maybe even something more. But prom didn't seem like the best place to discuss the future. Adrian deserved to enjoy his experience too, and I didn't plan to take that away from him.

Yet, there were still pressing things at hand, and I only had Felicia's attention for so long. Before she could but further distance between us, I reached out for her wrist in an effort to stop her.

"Wait, Felicia." I stopped in my tracks, all of a sudden lost in a trance about what I'd wanted to say. I wasn't sure how my words would be taken, but I worked up the courage to say them anyway. Whatever answer she gave, I'd just have to be satisfied with.

"Think we could talk later? After prom, I mean. I don't want to ruin your night. Or Adrian's. But I've been meaning to show you something back at The Unforgettable Spot. Like old time's sake," I half-pleaded, offering a weak, nervous smile, as I let go of her wrist.

I knew if her folks let her attend senior prom her junior year, she most likely had a curfew, so even if she did say yes, it'd be a hard sell.

A creeping silence passed between us, that I was glad we'd been on the balcony. The thrashing water diffused some of the awkward silence, and it didn't do much for my ego, considering I expected a "no" anyway.

"I don't know, Paul. I have to be home by ten-thirty, so I'm not in the position to promise you anything."

I nodded, half expecting her answer to be between that and no. "Okay. Well, I don't want to keep you if you wanted to look for Adrian. I hope you enjoy the rest of your night. I know I will," I concluded, as I involuntarily nodded again.

Felicia rolled on the ball of her heel, half to the door, half facing me. "I'll promise to try, Paul. If I'm not there by 10:45, I probably couldn't get out. I can't promise you much, but I'll at least promise to try," she finished, as she walked in the opposite direction toward the door, without so much as a glance back.

She promised she'd try. She could've said no; she probably wanted to. But there was no way to know, and I wasn't going to cause a downward spiral to my psyche trying to figure it out. A promise to try was all I could ask for. There was hope in trying.

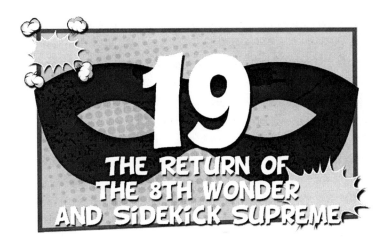

19

THE RETURN OF THE 8TH WONDER AND SIDEKICK SUPREME

PAUL

I stared out to the glistening lake, watching the moon caress the waves with its soft glow. As much as I missed Chicago, the year I spent in Portland reminded me that it wasn't a location that made a place home; it was the people.

This was my home now. And for the first time all year, I was going to miss it. I was going to miss her.

I sat here for nearly an hour, almost giving up on Felicia coming to meet me to talk. Maybe she wasn't coming. What did I expect? It's not like I didn't deserve it. I'd abandoned her. Something if I had the chance to take back, I would've in a heartbeat.

There was no way to turn back time, and I had to live with the decision I'd made that felt like ages ago. Nothing I'd ever felt in my life was as crappy as how I felt now. Nothing.

"Sorry, it took me so long. There was no way I was walking all the way here in that dress and shoes. I didn't know if you'd wait for me, but here you are, so..."

She approached me with her hands tucked in her jean pockets, face pointed to the ground. Seeing her in a change of clothes made me jealous that I hadn't stopped to think to go home first and throw on something less formal as well. Don't get me wrong, the gear was tight, but what I wouldn't give to be in a pair of shorts right now.

"So," I paused, "how was your date?" I asked in a way that could be mistaken as bitter. It didn't faze her, though. She sat down with her legs stacked on top of each other, and while the dry cleaning bill I'd end up paying to get this suit cleaned was going to kill me, I followed.

"Not as bad as I expected. I think next year I might actually try to, I don't know, participate in social society. As my alter ego, Felicia Abelard, of course. Not sure if it's a good idea to unveil thy true self," I laughed. Even after all this time, she was still an Unforgettable; she was still my Felicia.

"Plus, I think I might let softball and soccer take a back seat for my senior year. I wanted to get into some other things before I graduated, and sports take up too much of my time. Think I have what it takes to be a gleek?"

It was hard thinking of the right answer for that question. From the times I'd caught Felicia singing to herself when a pair of headphones saved her from the sound of her own voice, I couldn't help thinking I'd wished I had some too.

"I think maybe you should just stick to Drama or something. Your voice, Felicia, has *not* been crowd tested." She shoved me with her shoulder but stood up in front of me and reached for my hand.

"A trip to the secret lair, for old time's sake?" she asked. I really didn't want to get this suit wet, but if she was willing to submerge her hair underwater when it still looked really nice from earlier, the least I could do was follow in her footsteps.

"C'mon, 8th Wonder; don't be a sidekick." I took off my jacket before taking her hand in mine as she rushed me to the water. In one big cannonball, we were head deep beneath the lake, still holding hands, still the friends we were since that first swim last June. After we could no longer hold our breaths, we swam to the surface, spitting water from our laughing mouths as we made our way back to the shore.

We crashed down on the grass, wet and freezing, finding nothing but a blue-black sky with barely a moon as our only form of entertainment.

"I'm leaving for Illinois after graduation," I said to no one particular. I got accepted into The Art Institute of Chicago's summer program, and I'll be starting the fall semester soon after that. I guess that means we won't get much time to spend together before I leave."

"I'm happy for you," she said as a small smile formed at the side of her mouth, or maybe it was a full smile. At this angle, I couldn't tell.

"You are?"

She turned to face me. "Of course." Her eyes were expressive as they looked into mine. Her gaze as powerful as it was beautiful. *She* was beautiful.

"I'm going to miss you, Felicia," I said, trying to keep my emotions under control but failing miserably. I wiped away a few tears that formed at my eyes before she'd turn to me and take notice.

"Can we not focus on the "I'll miss yous" and "good-byes?" Just enjoy this time while we have it. Tonight doesn't have to be the end of something special but the beginning of something unforgettable." She paused.

"Man, I wish I had a pen or something. We could have used that as a catchphrase or something." We spent the next minute laughing and attempting to catch our breaths.

"The summer won't be the same without you."

She crawled up next to me and burrowed her head in the curve of my shoulder. I wrapped my arms around her, finding solace in the silence together. We'd decided that right now, there was no other place we'd rather be right now than right here. Together.

20

FELICIA FANTASTIC

All week, I'd watched how Paul prepared and packed for a summer and semester away from home. His siblings were already calling dibs on which one of them was moving in his room once he was gone, but I knew deep down the two of them were going to miss him. His plan was to not leave Maine without the things he deemed most important. That meant his art supplies and hat collection, which I'm pretty sure he was going to learn the hard way that packing his so-called essentials was going to be more hassle than it was worth, but even I couldn't convince him that some things were just better left behind.

He'd be the most stylish guy at SAIC. If that's the goal he was shooting for, he'd go far above and beyond. Who was anyone to stop him? Still, his mom pleaded with me to at least get him to leave the ten sets of sneakers he'd planned to pack. It was an argument I could only describe as combative and to the death. Not exactly something I wanted to experience. Ever again.

From my room, I could hear Paul downstairs joking with my parents, and from the strains in his voice, I knew they had to have been killing him in hugs. The moment was finally here. The time where we said our final goodbyes.

"Felicia," my mom yelled, "Paul is about to leave. Come downstairs and see him off, honey."

Taking one last glance in the mirror, I told myself to keep it together. To not cry. With the few weeks from his senior prom that led up to this moment, we'd made up for all the months we spent being resentful for what we couldn't be to each other. It was hard not being able to express our feelings for each other to the world, but it was even harder not being friends at all.

I missed the moments, the cheesy jokes, and the secret identities. Most of all, I missed him. I was willing to lock away my feelings if it meant things could be what they were, and for the past few weeks, they had been.

I rushed down the stairs to witness my folks preoccupied with gifts in their hands, flat and thin, most likely a drawing of some sort. My question was answered when Paul handed one to me, and it was then that I saw that it was a portrait. Not just any portrait. But a portrait of me.

He'd drawn me to be mystic and magical. Finding the perfect shade of brown to mimic my dark skin. And my hair was the wild, hypnotic mess that it was in person. I was whimsical and smiling, staring back at this creation he'd spent who knows how long slaving over.

In it, I was beautiful. Ethereally so. It had stolen the air around me at how breathtaking I found it.

"Do you like it?" he asked me. I so badly wanted to tell him yes, and yet the second my lips parted, there were no words good enough, powerful enough that truly encompassed how beautiful it was, how lucky I was to have him as a friend, and how sad I'd be to see him leave.

I knew this wasn't the end, but it was going to be farewell for a long time, and I wanted him to know. Wanted the world to know. Wanted my parents to know. Letting my heart lead the way to his lips, I did the one thing I'd held so much fear in my body to do. I kissed him.

With that kiss, I was free to finally be myself instead of the person I pretended so long that I was. I wasn't the perfect person and I wasn't the perfect daughter, and now I understood that that was okay. I had to start letting my heart guide me in the right direction, otherwise, I'd never find the bravery to do something like that again.

When I pulled away, silence had filled the room. In fact, it was so quiet, I was sure that my parents had perhaps walked off to give Paul and I some needed privacy. But nope. I turned around, and they were still watching. Still waiting. Most likely planning whether or not I'd be buried here in my hometown or some untraceable body of water off the coast of Haiti. With how they looked, all confused and soundless, I was positive that this was my last day on this planet.

"Mr. and Mrs. Abelard, please don't kill me, "Paul said, pleading, which only caused them to do the exact opposite. They broke out into a roar of laughter.

"Oh, Paul. We're going to miss having you around. Our daughter, well, she won't be the same without you."

My mom had let me walk him back outside, and we were met with his family jam-packed in their SUV.

"I left you something underneath your mattress. It was supposed to be for your birthday, but I don't want you to wait. I'd like for you to have it now."

"Well, do you want me to go get it and bring it down?" I asked, pointing towards my house, but I knew he had only seconds to spare before he had to leave.

"No, that's okay. I wanted it to be a surprise, but after what just happened in there, I just wanted you to see it. I've been working on it since last year so…yeah," he said as blood rushed to his face, and from then, he couldn't stop smiling.

"Okay, I guess you have to go now," I announced as disappointment transformed my once cheerful tone. He reached in and hugged me one last time before whispering, "I'll miss you." I watched their car reach the end of the street, but it wasn't until I saw their car leave out of view that I finally went back inside to rush to what he'd left for me back in my room.

It was a comic book, a comic book that you couldn't find on any shelf of any country because as far as I knew, was a Paul Hiroshima exclusive.

THE UNFORGETTABLES

THE ADVENTURES OF THE 8TH WONDER AND SIDEKICK SUPREME

I turned each page, astonished and amazed at how polished his second gift to me was. The artwork, the storyline. Even the humor was spot on. I found myself laughing at the adventures he'd chosen to capture with our given personas. And everyone made an appearance from what I could tell.

His mom was The Dictator, whom he'd drawn to resemble Olivier Armstrong from FullMetal Alchemist. She was a totalitarian ruler who sat regally on the base of her throne. And Daddy, whom he'd bestowed the name of Captain Crusader, conveniently looked a lot like Captain America but with a costume designed to mimic the Haitian flag. I had to admit that was pretty cool! I laughed at how he'd drawn his sister, or ahem The Prodigy, as just a human brain powered by stimulation in a rolling glass tank. And then there was me, Sidekick Supreme, which almost looked more awesome than the portrait he'd drawn of me.

Our superhero gear was contemporary, the way we dressed, only...Super. But when I got to the middle of our saga, there was a section marked as **BONUS CONTENT** and an editor's note to accompany it, all in Paul's sloppy, illegible handwriting.

244

NOTE TO READERS (OR *READER*)

This story started out as an ode to my love for comic books and the friendships I made in a new place far away from a place I called home. There I met a girl, who at first meeting, fought me over the one very thing that brought us together: comic books and superheroes.

She was a very special girl I was honored to call my best friend and partner in crime, but while this started as an ode to my love for all things geeky, it evolved into an ode for my love for her and what she's always been to me since that first time we locked eyes at that summer tag sale.

The next story is the end to the duo that was once *The Unforgettables,* featuring the title characters The 8th Wonder and Sidekick Supreme. Sidekick Supreme was always bigger than that. She deserved her own story. Most of all, I thought it was time for her to shed her old identity. So, from this day forth, it marks the start of a new chapter, a new brand of hero, one she was always destined to become.

THE BiRTH OF FELiCiA FANTASTiC

You'll always be my hero
Love Paul

ABOUT THE AUTHORS

Guinevere and Libertad go by so many superhero aliases, whether you know them by GL Tomas, The Twinjas, or the Rebellious Valkyries, their mission is always the same. Spreading awareness of diversity in books... Oh, and trying to figure out the use for pocket-less pants! They host other allies and champions of diversity in their secret lair in Connecticut.

Did you like/love this Young Adult title?

Consider subscribing to GL Tomas' YA newsletter
(https://tinyletter.com/RVPress)!

You'll get access to new content, releases,
and cover reveals before anyone else!

Want to know how we saw
The Unforgettables characters in their heads?

Check out The Unforgettables Pinterest board
(www.pinterest.com/rebelliousv/the-unforgettables-board).

Connect with us via Facebook
(https://www.facebook.com/TwinjaBookReviews?ref=hl)
and Twitter (https://twitter.com/Dos_Twinjas),
as we love to discuss diverse books!

We want to hear from you!
Write us at guinevere@gltomas.net
to discuss your fave stories by us!
Comments, Suggestions, even requests
what you'd like to see in our next publications!

Also if you loved this book, please consider leaving a review.
It really makes an author's day to read them and they're so, so
helpful in determining if this is the sort of read for the next
reader who may stumble across it.
And remember no review is too short!

ACKNOWLEDGEMENTS

First, we'd like to thank everyone who pushed us to write this title, including my sister (and obviously helped me write it) who helped pushed me to think it was worthy enough.

To our girl Kelsey. Thanks for convincing us that black people *actually* lived in Portland, Maine and prompting us to see it ourselves. Maine was the perfect setting for this story, we couldn't imagine it being any place else.

To Roger and Edward. Those translations really helped out and without y'all we wouldn't have been so in love anything and everything that has to do with Haiti. Especially the food. You know we can't forget the food, right?

Thanks to our awesome copy-editor, Patrice. I can't believe we were your first official Young Adult title. To many more with you! You were a pleasure to work with.

To Najla. Girl, you always slay us with your masterpieces. This cover you designed went above and beyond. We can never sleep after seeing the final product. This one was no different.

To Julie, our oh-so-talented formatter. You put so much thought into everything you create. It's always an honor to collaborate with you.

To Alice. We've known you for many years and we are always in awe of your talent. You brought our vision to life with so little details. It's like we have that psychic connection or something. Or maybe something close to it.

And last but not least, Geneva, our latest discovery. Your work is magical. Thanks for adding Felicia to your ranks of amazing portraits. May we work with you again someday!

MORE YA TITLES FROM G.L. TOMAS:

The Mark of Noba:
Book 1 of The Sterling Wayfairer Series
Available Now

A call of souls. Union of power. Transcendent of time.

Sterling Wayfairer has one goal for his senior year: make his mark. But things don't go as planned when he starts to encounter his mysterious classmate Tetra.

Tetra not only has answers to the recent disappearances, but Sterling will soon find, that making his mark isn't all it's cracked up to be.

Sterling discovers he shares a spiritual bond with Tetra, and that only their power has the ability to stop the malevolent evil they face. They must work together or risk the destruction of their world.

The City of Fallen Stars:
Book 2 of The Sterling Wayfairer Series
Coming Soon

CPSIA information can be obtained
at www.ICGtesting.com
Printed in the USA
LVOW12s1932070217
523493LV00005B/1046/P